D0312607

AUDITION & SUBTRACTION

ALSO BY AMY FELLNER DOMINY

OyMG

AUDITION & SUBTRACTION

Amy Fellner Dominy

WALKER & COMPANY
New York

First published in the United States of America in September 2012
by Walker Publishing Company, Inc., a division of Bloomsbury Publishing, Inc.
www.bloomsburykids.com

For information about permission to reproduce selections from this book, write to
Permissions, Walker BFYR, 175 Fifth Avenue, New York, New York 10010

Library of Congress Cataloging-in-Publication Data
Dominy, Amy Fellner.
Audition & subtraction / Amy Fellner Dominy.
p.   cm.
Summary: Tatum, a fourteen-year-old clarinetist, competes with new student Michael
for a spot in honor band, while trying to maintain her friendships and relationships.
ISBN 978-0-8027-2374-1
[1. Bands (Music)—Fiction. 2. Musicians—Fiction. 3. Interpersonal relationships—Fiction.
4. Friendship—Fiction. 5. Middle schools—Fiction. 6. Schools—Fiction.]
I. Title. II. Title: Audition and subtraction.
PZ7.D71184Au 2012   [Fic]—dc23   2011050973

Book design by Nicole Gastonguay
Typeset by Westchester Book Composition
Printed in the U.S.A. by Quad/Graphics, Fairfield, Pennsylvania
2 4 6 8 10 9 7 5 3 1

All papers used by Bloomsbury Publishing, Inc., are natural, recyclable products
made from wood grown in well-managed forests. The manufacturing processes
conform to the environmental regulations of the country of origin.

For Mary Koppen Vaughan
I would have survived middle school
without you, but I'm not sure how

AUDITION & SUBTRACTION

♪ 1 ♫

Death by bikini." I looked at Lori, who stood by the door of my bedroom. "You can put that on my grave when I die of embarrassment today." I dangled last year's bikini top from my fingers, the material so faded it was practically see-through.

She sighed and shook her head. "You're just looking for a swimsuit now? We have to leave in ten minutes."

Early-morning sun poured through my bedroom window. It was only the beginning of April, but in Phoenix it already felt like summer. We'd probably get a tan at the band car wash. Well, Lori would get a tan, and I'd get arrested for indecent exposure.

"I didn't think it was so faded." I shoved the top back in my dresser drawer.

"You should have come with me to the mall last night," she said, fingering the neck strap of her new pink bikini.

"I couldn't. I had to go to Dad's." I shuddered. As if I needed reminding of that on top of everything else. I rubbed a hand over my face. Was that a frown line between my eyes? Was I face-scrunching in my sleep? Great. One more thing to stress about—wrinkles in middle school.

"Girls?" Mom's voice floated up the stairs. "You about ready?"

"In a minute," I called down. Mr. Van Sant had dropped off Lori so my mom could drive us there together. Now we were going to be late. "I just won't wear a suit."

"It's a car wash. You have to." Lori dropped her purse and knelt next to me, riffling through my drawer. I didn't mention that *she'd* never worn a suit to a car wash before. Or a bikini *ever*. Up until now, she'd worn a one-piece suit with a T-shirt over—even when it was just the two of us in the backyard swimming. Sometimes I couldn't help flashing back to how things were before she'd lost weight. I wondered if Lori was thinking about it, too, since I'd seen her touch her neck strap a few times.

"Here," she said, pulling out a suit I'd worn for the sixth-grade swim team. "Wear this."

"Are you kidding?" I said. "It's hideous."

"It is not."

"I cannot meet *him* wearing *that*."

Him was Michael Malone. He'd transferred to Dakota Middle School last week, but he didn't officially start until Monday. None of us had met him yet, but he'd be at the car wash today. And I wasn't about to face the enemy in a one-piece with a logo that said A PORPOISE WITH A PURPOSE.

"Girls?" Mom called, her voice edged with impatience.

"One minute!" I yelled back.

Lori pressed the suit into my hand. "You'll look great, Tay."

I groaned, but how could I say no when it was so important to Lori? I wouldn't want to make a bikini debut on my own, either. I grabbed the rest of my clothes and went into the connecting bathroom. The door on the other side was open—it led to Andrew's bedroom. I wrinkled my nose at the lingering smell of his new cologne. Emily, his girlfriend, had bought it for his sixteenth birthday, and the whole top floor stunk like musk. The smell bugged me, but not as much as Andrew's open door. I didn't want a reminder that he'd spent the night at Dad's. He shouldn't have. It made the separation feel more . . . permanent.

And it wasn't.

I slipped on the suit, sucking in my breath to get the straps over my shoulders. Last year the suit had been small, but this year it felt like shrink-wrap. Good-bye, cleavage, not that I had much to begin with. I pulled on my red band tee and blue shorts, same as Lori. "We're working the money table, so I won't have to take off my shirt anyway," I called through the open door.

"Would you quit worrying?" she said.

I sighed, as all the things I'd been worrying about wormed their way back into my brain. "I wish I didn't have to."

There was a heartbeat of silence from the bedroom, and I knew Lori understood.

Michael Malone. He was a clarinet player—same as me. Apparently he was good. Really good. According to Mr. Wayne, our band director, Michael had been invited to play with a youth symphony in Dallas, Texas. I'd never even *heard* a youth symphony before. And now here he was, ready to take part in all band activities.

Including auditions for District Honor Band.

I heard the mattress squeak, and a second later Lori stood at the bathroom door. "No dweeb from Texas is going to take your spot."

I had to smile. Lori played flute, so the new guy wasn't competition for her. But as my best friend, she'd promised to hate him, too. Just to be nice.

"You're good, Tay. You've been playing amazing this whole year."

Lori was the amazing one—really, truly talented. But maybe I'd been playing better these past few months. I'd been practicing a ton, and it had to count that I wanted it so much. Some new guy couldn't just move in and take my place.

Unless he is better than me.

Only three clarinet players from each middle school

could make District Honor Band, and there were seven of us in the section. Brooke wasn't auditioning because her family always went back East the last weekend of May when the concert was scheduled. I still had Angie and Aaron ahead of me, and they'd make it for sure. That left only *one* open spot. The spot I'd been counting on.

I rubbed a hand over my stomach. The words "youth symphony" were swirling like acid in my gut. "I think I'm getting an ulcer over this. I'm not sure what a bleeding ulcer is, but I may have one of those, too."

"You don't have an ulcer. Now, would you hurry?"

I quickly wound a rubber band through my thick hair, pulling it into a ponytail. If only I had Lori's hair—it did all the things mine wouldn't, like lie flat against my head. Her French braid looked way prettier than my boring pony—maybe I could try that later. I studied my face, wishing my eyes weren't so tired and puffy. At least mascara would help. Unscrewing the wand, I swept it up and under, but my lashes were smashed from sleeping. I tried again and a shot of pain ripped through me.

"Ow!" I cried.

"What?" Lori asked.

"I stabbed myself with the mascara wand." I blinked open my eye. A million veins were now throbbing red across it. "Veins on eyeballs? Whose idea was that?"

"At least it matches your shirt," Lori offered.

"Perfect. I always like to color-coordinate with my eyeball."

She grinned, then stood next to me in front of the mirror. Our eyes met in the glass, and she bumped my shoulder with hers. "He's not going to be better than you. I promise. I won't let him be."

I smiled, this time for real. Lori had changed so much in the past few months, but her blue eyes were the same, and today they were so full of certainty I couldn't help but feel better. If anyone could promise me a spot in District Honor Band, Lori could. She wasn't just my best friend. She was my duet partner for auditions.

I bumped her shoulder in return. "So let's go meet the dweeb."

When Mom dropped us at the Chevron station, the other Bandies were already there and everything had been set up. I looked around but no sign of a geek in a cowboy hat.

Aaron and Tanner were unfolding a table and chairs under the shade of a tree. By the back wall of the station, everyone else had gathered with hoses and supplies. Lori and I headed that way, our matching flip-flops smacking the pavement in rhythm.

"Tay-Lo!" Kerry called as she waved us over. Kerry

had given us the nickname back in fourth grade, because it was quicker than saying Tatum and Lori, and we were always together anyway. Kerry and Misa were mixing soap into buckets of water. They were our next best friends, and we'd all signed up to work the car wash together.

"He's not here yet," Kerry said.

Everyone was curious about the new guy. Mr. Wayne had made a big deal about us all welcoming him because it was difficult transferring so close to graduation. Maybe it wasn't fair for me to hate him right off. He had to be nervous and—

Misa gasped, her gaze fixed on something behind me. "Ooh, baby," she whispered. "I hope that's him!"

♪ 2 ♫

The guy heading our way on a skateboard was no dweeb. At least not from the outside. Tallish, with dark hair long enough to catch the breeze, he rode the board like an athlete, dipping low to hop a curb. The untied laces of his black Chucks flapped like streamers behind him.

I looked at Lori, but she didn't look back. She was staring at the new guy along with everyone else.

"Dang," Kerry said. "They make 'em hot in Texas."

"Good-bye, band geek; hello, rock star," Misa added.

So, yeah, he was cute—if you liked guys who moved in at the last minute and threatened to take your place in District Honor Band. Which I didn't. I yanked at the strap of my suit and tried to breathe.

Michael had spotted us now—it was hard to miss our group with Mr. Wayne waving both arms in the air and calling his name. He must have known we were all staring, but he didn't seem nervous. He rode up to Mr. Wayne, spraying gravel as he skidded to a stop. "Hey, Coach," he said.

Coach? No one called Mr. Wayne Coach, but he grinned as if he could get used to it. "Welcome, Mr. Malone," he said, his cheeks nearly as red as his band T-shirt. Mr. Wayne is a big man—especially in the gut. Some kids make fun of him, but none of us ever would. He's the coolest band director ever, and once you know him, you forget all about how he looks.

"Glad you could join us," he added.

Michael looked around, giving everyone a half smile and a nod. "Hey."

I swear Kerry stopped breathing.

Mr. Wayne introduced us, and I stood there praying my suit wouldn't snap like a rubber band. I wanted to look cool and confident, but that's hard when you haven't had a full breath in twenty minutes and you're sweaty and purple in the face. Purple is not my best color.

"This is Jenny," Mr. Wayne said. "Our first trombone player."

Jenny had a heavy coil of green hose slung over her shoulder, but she still managed a shrug.

"Misa plays flute, and Kerry plays saxophone."

Misa smiled while Kerry fixed him with her gaze and fluttered her eyelashes in a move she'd been perfecting since fourth grade when her aunt said she had lovely eyelashes the color of soot. We'd had to look up the word "soot," and even though it meant powdery smoke residue, Kerry thought it sounded glamorous.

"José is on percussion," Mr. Wayne went on. "Tanner and Brandon—trumpet. Aaron—clarinet." Then he nodded to where we stood. "Tatum also plays clarinet, and Lori is our principal flute."

We both sort of nodded, and he smiled, his sunglasses reflecting back my face for a second before moving to Lori. His smile widened, and she shuffled from one foot to the other. I was still half behind her, and I tapped her with my shoulder.

Loser, right? my shoulder nudge said.

She didn't nudge back.

"So," Mr. Wayne was saying, "that's the crew for today. If we all—"

A loud motor rumbled up, drowning out his voice. The sharp smell of gas and asphalt rose as a red truck smeared with mud chugged past the gas pumps and stopped beside the hoses.

"That's my dad," Jenny said.

"Excellent!" Mr. Wayne clapped his hands like he was starting band practice. "We have our first customer, people. Who's doing what?"

"Misa and I will do windows," Kerry said.

"I'll run the hose," Jenny offered.

Tanner grabbed a towel off the stack. "Me and Brandon will dry."

"I got wheels," José said, stuffing his drumsticks in his back pocket. He took his drumsticks everywhere— including the bathroom.

I raised my hand. "Money table."

"I'll wash," Michael said. Then he looked right at Lori. "You want to wash with me?"

I think I gasped, but it might have been Kerry, because her mouth had dropped open far enough that I could see the hangy thing in the back of her throat.

"What? Um . . ." Lori's cheeks flushed brick red as she turned to look at me. "I'm already . . . uh . . ."

"She's doing money table with me," I said.

"I can wash after I put up the signs," Aaron offered.

Michael tilted his chin in a micro nod. " 'Kay."

"Well, then, everyone," Mr. Wayne said impatiently. "Get busy!"

There was a quick exchange of looks among Kerry, Misa, Lori, and me, but no time to talk. Jenny already had the hose going, and her dad was handing Mr. Wayne money.

Lori grabbed my arm and led me toward the table. Two metal chairs had been set up, half on asphalt and half on gravel so we could sit in the shade of the tree. "I am such an idiot," she hissed.

"What?"

"Did you hear me back there? So embarrassing."

Before I could say anything, Mr. Wayne strode over waving a stack of bills. "Our first donation."

"Cool," I said. "Thanks." I pulled the gray metal cash

box closer as I sat down. Lori sat next to me, grinding her chair into the gravel. I opened the box and slid the bills under a metal clip.

By now, Jenny had sprayed the truck, and Michael was running a soapy rag along the front hood.

"So much for him being a dweeb, huh?" I said.

"Kerry's going to wear out her eyelashes," Lori muttered.

"He hardly even noticed her. You're the one he was staring at."

She combed her bangs with her fingertips. "I was not."

"He asked you to wash with him."

"I was the only one left."

"Aaron was left."

"It just . . . I wasn't . . . Oh snap," she muttered. "I'm doing it again."

Lori always got nervous around guys. I didn't blame her—guys had been major jerks to her for years. But no one was going to tease her about being fat now. Not that she'd been fat-fat or anything. Just sort of heavy. Then, in January, she got a bad case of stomach flu that lasted a week. She lost over eight pounds from being sick. Instead of gaining it back, she got serious about eating healthy and kept losing more. She'd always been pretty, but in the past few months, she'd turned beautiful. Way more beautiful than I'd ever be.

It's not that I'm unfortunate looking. I have nice

green eyes, my nose is bump-free, and my skin is so dry I never get zits. But my hair is an unnatural disaster. Basic brown and so thick I could double as a wooly mammoth. I've always been thin, but guys have never stared at me the way they do Lori. The way Michael stared when he first saw her.

The way he's staring right now.

I bumped her knee with mine. "He's watching you."

"He is not," she said. But the tips of her ears flared pink. "He's wearing sunglasses. You can't tell what he's looking at."

"You're wearing sunglasses, and I can tell that you're looking at him."

She bumped my knee back, only harder. "If I am," she said, "it's just because I'm surprised. He's cute."

"I don't know," I said. "Don't you think he looks dumb with his shoelaces untied?"

"No. And ssshhh," she added, turning to make sure no one was paying attention.

Nobody was. Aaron had grabbed the car-wash signs and disappeared around the front of the station. Everyone else was busy scrubbing mud off the truck. "If he didn't play clarinet, you'd think he was cute," she said.

A sudden squeal came from the washing area. A second later, Misa sprinted out from behind the truck, her shirt soaking wet and half of one arm dripping. Tanner followed her, wiping water out of his eyes, his shirt already off. Kerry high-fived Michael like he was her BFF.

"Kerry doesn't even know him. He could be a serial killer," I said. "Ted Bundy was cute, and he was a serial killer."

"See, you do think he's cute," Lori said with a grin. "Hey, look," she added. "Kerry's waving us over. You want to go?"

"And wash? No." I paused. "Why? Do you?"

"I don't know. Maybe."

"Because of Michael Malone?"

Her shoulders stiffened. "Not because of him."

"Good. Because he's a potential serial killer."

She gave me one of her patented double eye-rolls. "You watch too much History Channel."

I tried to double eye-roll back, but it made my eye sockets hurt. "Even if he isn't a deranged psychopath, I thought we were going to hate him."

"We can hate him while we wash cars."

"Seriously?" I said. "You want to go wash cars?"

"It would be a good way to pump him for information about where he sat in his old band." She gave me a pointed look.

"I guess," I said. "But I've got to stay with the money."

"Aaron can do it."

A white SUV pulled in, country music blaring from the open window. Misa had just peeled off her shirt. Kerry, too. Their suits were flattering. Mine was flattening. "No, I'll stay."

"Do you care if I go?" Her eyes flickered toward Michael and then back at me.

I forced a shrug. "If you want to . . ."

She pushed back her chair. "You're sure?"

"Yeah, I'm sure." But before I'd gotten the words out, she was already gone.

♪ 3 ♫

You alone?" Aaron's shoes crunched on the gravel as he walked over.

"Lori decided to wash for a few," I said. "Aren't you supposed to be doing signs?"

He slid into her chair and dragged it closer to the table. "I bungee-corded them to the light posts."

Aaron wore green gym shorts and a red T-shirt that said EINSTEIN WAS A SPACE CADET, TOO. He wasn't a loser—he just dressed like one. I couldn't imagine Aaron with his shoelaces untied. He had a nice face, not that you could see all of it. His reddish-brown hair always hung halfway over his eyes, though today he'd stuffed it under a baseball hat.

"So how much have we made?" he asked, opening the metal box.

"Fifteen dollars." I watched two more cars pull

around. Jenny turned on the hose, and there were shrieks as the water sprayed wild for a second. Lori stood in the middle of it all. It was like looking at someone I didn't know, some pretty girl with shiny blond hair and a wet T-shirt, laughing so hard even I could hear her. How could that be Lori? When had she ever wanted to be in the middle of anything without me being there, too?

Mr. Wayne walked over with a stack of one-dollar bills. "From the SUV driver," he said, handing it to Aaron.

"Nice," Aaron said. Instead of charging a set amount, we were asking for donations. So far, it seemed to be paying off. He waved the bills at me. "I'm guessing we can make big bucks. Look, another customer."

A blue van pulled up. Michael grabbed his board and a wet rag and skated along the side of the van, washing as he went. Then his wheels hit a towel someone had dropped and he flipped off. Lori busted up.

"You think that's funny?" I heard him say. Then he grabbed a bucket and launched a sheet of soapy water at her. She screamed and turned, but she was laughing her butt off.

Her eyes flashed over my way.

I half waved.

She peeled the wet bangs off her face and said something to Kerry. Then she ran toward the money table. Unexpected relief washed through me—she was coming back.

She stopped short of the table, breathing hard. A line of soap dripped off her shoulder. "You good here?" Before I could answer, she yanked off her shirt. "Keep this for me?" With a wide smile, she dropped the shirt on the table. "Thanks!"

I watched her race back, her flip-flops leaving wet prints like a trail I couldn't follow.

"Go wash," Aaron said softly. "I got this."

I lifted my shoulders for a shrug, but that only reminded me of the suit under my tee. I'd look stupid wearing my shirt when everyone else was in a bikini. "I will in a while," I said as I hung Lori's shirt over the back of my chair.

Aaron nodded even though I could tell he didn't believe me. Which was okay. Aaron was pretty cool. I'd known him forever, but this past year we'd gotten to be good friends. Sometimes I wanted to punch him for always being so smart, but mostly he was easy to be around.

He finished counting out the dollar bills in the box. "So the new guy seems okay."

"I guess." I slouched back in my chair. "I just wish he didn't play clarinet."

"You'll make District Honor Band," he said. "You made it last year."

"Barely." I chewed at the inside of my cheek. Aaron didn't have anything to worry about. He'd finished first last year. I'd eked out third place—by *one* point! The only reason I'd done that well was because I had Lori as my duet partner. I got nervous on my own, but Lori was so good she made me sound good, too.

The funny part was that *I* had talked Lori into band in the first place. My mom had signed me up for clarinet lessons when I was ten. I figured the music experiment would turn out like the ballet lessons, cheerleading camp, YMCA soccer, and tumbling—in other words, humiliating.

Instead, I loved it. I loved how solid the clarinet felt in my hands, the smell of the reed, and how my fingers could turn notes on a page into actual music.

Lori decided on the flute, and wouldn't you know— she turned out to be a natural. I tried not to let it bother me that it came so easily for her. Besides, even if you're not a natural, that doesn't mean you can't make up for it by working harder. But sometimes, I still worried that no matter how much I practiced, it wouldn't be enough.

Next year, most of us would go to Adobe High, and kids like Lori and Aaron would make Wind Ensemble, the school's top performance band. They'd go on to be selected for Regionals and even All-State. Me, I'd probably end up in Concert Band, the basic, no-cut band. I'd be one of those kids who was good, but not good enough.

Maybe that was why District Honor Band felt so important. It was my chance to sit on that stage with everyone as if I were a natural—and not just someone who wanted to be. Up until a week ago, I'd been pretty sure I could squeak out the third spot again. But that was before Mr. Youth Symphony showed up.

No wonder I was face-scrunching in my sleep.

I blinked as a kid ran over wearing SpongeBob pajamas and waving money. He paid Aaron with two crumpled five-dollar bills. Aaron wiped the jelly off one of them.

"If you're worried," Aaron said, "you should do a solo."

I fake shivered. "I'd rather eat out of a litter box."

"You score higher with a solo," he pointed out.

"Not if you pass out in the middle of it."

"You won't pass out!"

"No," I agreed, "because I'm not doing a solo. Besides, I don't need to. Lori's my secret weapon."

I paused while a woman with pigtails, overalls, and orange platform sandals walked up. Then she paid with a twenty and refused any change, so I forced my eyebrows back into place. It didn't feel right to make fun of her.

I studied Michael as he soaped up another car. "He doesn't look like he'd be that good."

Aaron adjusted the brim of his hat. "You can tell that from a car wash?"

"No," I said. "But he's got pouty lips. That's bad for the embouchure."

"Pouty lips?"

"Yeah." I shoved him with the heel of my hand.

Aaron laughed. "Do I have pouty lips?" He puckered like a blowfish.

"No."

"So what kind of lips do I have?" He puckered again.

"I'm not some kind of lip expert," I said. But I looked anyway. At his lips. It was no big deal except I suddenly thought about how in movies right before a big kiss, the girl looks at the guy's lips, and then there's this pause. And here I was, looking at Aaron's lips, and there was a pause.

Heat flooded my cheeks at the whole weirdness of it. "I don't know," I said, looking away. "You have regular lips. Clarinet lips."

"Clarinet lips?"

"Yeah. From practicing all the time."

"You want to know about your lips?"

"No." I folded my arms over my middle. "Can we stop talking about lips?"

"You brought them up," he said.

"I was asking if you thought Michael would be any good." I shifted to face him. "Aren't you worried that he might be better than you?"

"Yeah," he admitted. "But we won't know until Monday when he auditions for Mr. Wayne. Why freak out about it now?"

"Because that's what normal people do," I said. "Not that you'd know that because you're a freak."

Aaron grinned. He was impossible to insult. In fact, Aaron actually *was* a freaking genius. He was in all my honors classes, plus the only guy in science club to build a rocket that actually launched.

My ears registered a laugh just then, and my eyes tried to follow. Lori was doubled over with laughter as Michael said something. I wished I could read lips. A deaf person would know exactly what he was saying, but to me it looked like "pickle wee chicken."

"If Mr. Wayne does put him behind us, I hope he's not a spitter," Aaron said. "You never know with those *pouty lips*."

I smacked him.

"Ow," he said, pretending to be hurt. "You better watch it, or I won't share the extra cash with you."

"What extra cash?"

"The extra cash we're going to collect for a tub of Baskin-Robbins brownie chunk ice cream."

I glanced behind us. I could see the Baskin-Robbins sign in the strip center. I couldn't see how we were going to get the money, though. "You can't take it from the cash box. That's stealing."

He gave me a hurt look. "I wouldn't steal from the band."

"So where are you getting the money?"

"People are going to give it to us."

"Why would they?"

"Because we're cute."

I laughed. He actually did look cute with his hat on crooked and his hair sticking out around his neck. "We're too old to be cute," I said.

"You don't believe me, then watch."

I settled back in my chair, curious. Besides, it was better than trying to read Michael's lips and wondering why Misa and Kerry kept sending me thumbs-up signs.

Another lady made her way to the table, a wad of ones in her hand.

"Thanks," Aaron said, taking the money. "Would you consider contributing to our dairy fund?"

Her brows knit together. "What's that?"

"Well," he said, a serious expression on his face, "we spend hours with instruments in our mouths, and it's really hard on our teeth. In fact, it can cause horrible disfigurement." He flashed her a smile that showed off his braces. "See what I mean?"

Her lips twitched at the corners.

He nudged me, and I opened my mouth, pointing to the metal retainer glued to my bottom teeth—the remains of two years of dental torture.

The twitch turned into a smile.

Aaron folded his hands together and went on. "Scientists, working around the clock to help save band members across the country, have discovered that large doses of dairy products could strengthen teeth and prevent this horrible plague."

A grin had worked its way across her face. "A plague, huh?"

Aaron nodded. "It's worse than plaque."

The lady laughed. So did I. That was pretty quick, even for Aaron.

"Fortunately, there's a Baskin-Robbins over there," he finished.

She shook her head, but she pulled a dollar from her bag. "Cute. Very cute. You should go into sales."

Aaron took the dollar. "Thanks."

After she walked off, I grabbed the dollar from his hand. "I can't believe you just did that!"

"What did I tell you? Cute. Very cute."

I sat back and waited for the next customer, still smiling. Wait until I told Lori.

Then I glanced her way and caught her standing on Michael's skateboard. Lori? On a skateboard? I blinked as if I could bring her back into focus. Because Lori on a skateboard . . . never. At least, never before.

A second later, Lori wobbled backward and shrieked as she fell off. The board shot out, and Michael caught it. The others all applauded.

"He's kind of a show-off, isn't he?" I said.

Aaron shrugged. "Lori doesn't seem to mind."

"She's supposed to be spying," I muttered. "For me." Only, it didn't exactly look that way.

A breeze swirled up out of nowhere. Aaron grabbed a loose dollar bill that fluttered in the cash box. It was a warm breeze, but I still shivered. I couldn't help it. It made me think of something my dad used to say.

The Winds of Change.

It was his favorite expression when I was little. He'd hold up a finger as if to feel the breeze. As if there really were Winds of Change. And then we would move to a new state. We moved from California to Colorado to New Mexico and then to Arizona. I hated moving, hated new cities and new schools and new friends. For a long time, I didn't understand it was because of Dad's job as a pilot—I really thought it was the wind. Because of that, I grew up afraid of storms. Every time one came, I worried that a wind would blow in, and off we would go like some creepy version of Mary Poppins.

Dad hadn't held up a finger to test the breeze when he and Mom announced they were separating. But he might as well have. Everything had changed. And I hated it. I hated every threatening gust of newness.

I watched Lori and Michael and shivered again.

♪ 4 ♫

In the fifty-two days since Dad had loaded two suit-cases in his truck and drove off, my house had become a weird place to be.

Except for Saturday nights.

Every Saturday night, Lori slept over. It was the one time when things felt normal. We ordered pizza for dinner, watched movies, and stayed up late, talking.

Tonight, Lori hadn't come over until after dinner because she had to watch Katie, her little sister. And this afternoon, she'd gone right from the car wash to her private flute lesson. So it was after nine o'clock, and we still hadn't talked about the day.

Or *him*.

Finally, it was just the two of us in my room. Lori sat on the pop-up trundle, and I sat across from her, a plate of brownies I'd baked that afternoon between us.

I'd turned off the light, but my room glowed so much we could see each other fine. Lori said my room at night felt like the inside of an alien spaceship. My bedside clock gleamed with green letters, and my night-light flashed red, green, and blue. Plus, on the ceiling, a galaxy of stick-on stars shone down on us.

I loved stars. I always had. When I grew up, I wanted to be an astronomer. I was going to discover a new solar system and name the stars after all my friends. Lori would get first pick.

She leaned back, resting her weight on her hands, and let out an exaggerated sigh. I knew the feeling. No matter what had happened during the day, when we were hanging out just the two of us, I could let down my guard and just *be*.

"So why did you have to watch Katie?" I asked.

"My parents." She wore a long gray sleep shirt with NEW YORK PHILHARMONIC in black lettering. I wore the same one, only in blue. Lori had brought it back for me after her trip last summer.

"It's so humiliating," she said. "They started dance lessons."

"Seriously?"

"At the studio next to Dominic's Pizza. The one with all the big windows, so the world can see my dad step on my mom's feet."

I imagined my parents dancing out in public, but instead of horror, I felt a stab of sadness. "At least your parents are there together."

Her eyes glowed a dark blue in the alien light. "Sorry, Tay. Anything new with your mom and dad?"

I shook my head. "I don't know how they're supposed to work things out if they never talk."

"Maybe they'll miss each other more that way."

"Mom misses him enough already. I heard her crying again yesterday." I picked the edge off a brownie and let the chocolate melt on my tongue. "If she'd just leave him alone about his job, he'd come home."

"Except he wasn't home much, right?"

"It was still better than this," I grumbled. Being a pilot for FedEx meant Dad was gone a few nights every week. But after six years, it was part of the routine. And then this new job came along—corporate pilot for some software company in China. No more night flights, better pay, and Dad would get to fly a Gulfstream 5, whatever that was. But it meant he'd be gone a lot more—sometimes a month at a time. I figured that's what had started the separation talk.

"At least they're not using the D word, right?" Lori asked.

"You mean the D *words*?" I said. "Because there are a bunch." I ticked them off on my fingers. "Divorce. Dissolve. Disintegrate. Demolish. Destroy."

"I'm sorry, Tay. Honest. I wish I could do something."

"I know," I said. "I wish there were something I could do, too."

I'd tried pretending Dad was just working. But the

house felt weird, because stuff that used to be there suddenly wasn't. Mom snuck into the laundry room to cry, and Andrew acted like everything was fine, but even he walked around the house as if he were looking for something but forgot where he put it.

Why can't Dad just come home?

I blinked back tears, suddenly so glad Lori was there. "We have to stop talking about this before I go insane. Tell me about today, instead." I shifted, careful not to wobble the plate. "What's the new guy like?"

She shrugged, but the corners of her mouth twitched, and I wondered if she knew she was smiling. "It's hard to be sure, but he seemed pretty cool."

She'd left her braid in, but more wispy pieces had pulled loose. I'd tried to braid mine this afternoon, but so much hair stuck out I looked like the victim of an electrical shock.

"Did you talk about band stuff?"

"A little." She broke off the corner of a brownie. "He's definitely auditioning for District Honor Band."

"He said that?"

She nodded. "I guess music is a big deal in his family. His parents are divorced, and his dad plays trombone in an orchestra in New York."

"Wow." My throat tightened. "So he's good, huh?"

"Maybe," she admitted. "But he also said he's only been serious for about two years. Except . . ." She reached for more brownie, then stopped and crossed her arms over her chest.

"Except what?"

"You have to keep those brownies away from me. You shouldn't have made them in the first place."

"I know, but we always used to make brownies every Saturday. Remember? I figured one brownie wouldn't kill us."

"I'm not worried about dying. I'm worried about fat thighs."

"You don't have fat thighs."

"I do, too. Michael showed me a scar on his leg, and all I could think about was how my thighs are nearly as big as his."

"He showed you a scar? On his leg?" I made a face as I stuck the plate on my bedside table.

She rolled her eyes. "It wasn't bloody and scabbed over. It was just an old scar by his knee. He has nice knees," she added. "They're not all skinny and white."

"Nice *kneeees*?" I said, drawing out the word.

Lori's mouth tightened.

"What?" I said. "I'm just joking."

"Well, it's not funny."

"Sorry," I said, but it felt like she'd changed the rules of a game without telling me. This morning she'd promised to hate Michael as much as I did—and suddenly she liked his knees? But I let it go, and instead I said, "So go back a minute. What did you mean—*except*. Except what?"

She twisted the end of her braid around one finger. "His mom already looked into the program at Adobe

High for next year. He knows about Dr. Hallady and the Wind Ensemble."

"He wants to be in Wind Ensemble?"

She nodded again. "He even asked me about summer music camps. Plus," she added, leaning forward, "it turns out he was at the New York Philharmonic last June, the exact same time when I was there. And get this—Mozart is his favorite composer, too."

"You asked him his favorite composer?"

"No," she said, her eyes widening. "He asked me mine!"

"Wow." I wrapped my arms around my knees. "Okay." I wasn't really sure what to say. "Freakingtastic" was the only thing that came to mind.

Then her lips stretched into a slow, secret smile. "He asked for my phone number. He typed it right into his cell."

"You gave it to him?" My stomach flipped in a not-so-good way. "Did you ask for his number?"

"No." She sat up a little straighter. "Was I supposed to?"

"I don't know. If you liked him, I guess. I mean, do you like him?"

"I only just met him."

"Then why did you give him your cell number?"

"I was just being nice." She rolled onto her stomach, pulling a pillow beneath her chin. "Besides, I might like him in the future."

"So now you're planning to like him?"

"I don't know," she said. "What does it even mean to like a guy? Misa likes Sam, and they break up every other week. Kerry says she likes Caleb, but not enough to wear the necklace he got her."

"It was a skeleton head. I wouldn't wear it, either."

"You know what I mean."

"Yeah," I admitted. "It would be easier if it were scientific. Like a math formula that told you if you liked a guy." I grabbed my pillow and slid onto my stomach until I was even with Lori. "Good smile + cute butt × sense of humor = Like."

Lori laughed. "It's too bad Mr. Phillips doesn't teach that kind of math."

I nodded. "There could be equations for different levels of like."

"Levels of like?"

"Because there are different ways to like a guy."

Lori grinned. "So, what would Level One be?"

"Level One," I said, thinking a second, "is when you like a guy as a friend."

"Sort of like you and Aaron?"

"Yeah," I said. "Level One means no kissing. Ever. Unless it's a funeral or something, because everyone kisses at funerals." I suddenly thought about Aaron puckering today and his lips. . . . Then I flashed on the two of us at a funeral . . . Aaron leaning in close . . .

I shook off the thought. *Okay, super awkward.*

"What's Level Two?" Lori asked.

"Level Two is when you *maybe* like a guy."

She gathered her pillow into a hug. "Or when you *could* maybe like him—as in future potential."

"Exactly," I said. "Which means Level Three is the highest level, and that's when you *like-like* a guy. He's all you ever think about, and you get nervous just being around him."

"And when he smiles, you want to scream," Lori said.

"And when he kisses you, you want to faint."

Lori shuddered. "I would hate to faint. Just all of a sudden fall over?"

"Yeah," I agreed. "You'd hit the floor and break bones. And I'm guessing there would be drool involved."

"It would have to be a really good kiss," she said.

Neither one of us had ever been kissed. I figured Lori would be first now that she'd turned beautiful. "Remember," I said, "if you ever kiss a guy, you promise to tell me before anyone else."

"And you, too." Her eyes glowed like minilanterns. "But I'm not kissing anyone anytime soon. It was just a car wash, Tay. Once Michael gets to school on Monday, Stace and Alesia will be all over him."

"You're nicer, smarter—and prettier than they are, too."

"I am not," she said, ducking her head. But I could still see her smile.

"So are you and Michael Level One?" I asked, my breath catching as I waited for her answer.

She gave an easy shrug. "Definitely."

I resumed breathing as she glanced back toward my closet. "You mind if I try on your jeans? I want to see if they fit."

"Now?" I said. "Okay."

"Andrew's not going to walk in on us, is he?"

I shook my head. "He's at Emily's."

A second later, she flipped through the stack of jeans I kept on a shelf in the closet.

"If they fit, can I wear them on Monday? Just for something different."

"Sure."

She pulled a pair of jeans loose and shimmied into them under her sleep shirt.

"Brandon is having a party," I said. "At the hotel during Band Night Out."

"As if I care what that idiot is doing."

Brandon was one of the guys who'd made fun of Lori's weight all through grade school. He made fun of my hair, too, but I still wanted to go to his party.

A second later she turned, wearing my faded jeans with a rip over the right knee. She held her sleep shirt bunched in one hand and smoothed the other hand over her hips. "They almost fit." She stared at herself in the mirror hanging on my closet door. "He doesn't know I was fat."

"Huh?" She'd spoken so softly, at first I wasn't sure I'd heard her.

"Michael," she said, still looking at herself. "Everyone else in the whole school still sees me as the fat girl who lost weight. To him, I'm just thin. You can tell by the way he looks at me."

I didn't get what she meant, but I nodded like I did. As far as I could tell, everyone looked at her now like she was thin.

She slid out of my jeans and set them on her pile of stuff under my desk. "What a great day," she said, climbing back into bed.

"It's going to be an awesome last two months—Band Night Out and then summer vacation."

"Don't forget District Honor Band," she said. "We'll get to perform at the downtown art center."

I crossed my fingers. "If I still make it."

"You will," she said. "How's the duet coming?"

"Okay, but I do better when we practice together."

"We will. First you have to get the notes down." She yawned, and it made me yawn, too.

"I've got brownies in my teeth," I said.

"Yeah," she agreed. "Me, too."

We slid out of bed and went into the bathroom. We stood over the sink, brushing until both of us had white foam spilling out of our mouths. We spit at the same time, which would have been disgusting with anyone but Lori. I pointed to the sink. "Does that remind you of anything?"

"Curdled milk?"

"That, too, but I was thinking of the day I threw up on your sandals."

She half groaned, half laughed. "That was the worst."

"Yeah," I agreed. "But it was also the best."

That was the day we met for the first time. It was also the first day of third grade. We'd just moved to Phoenix, and I knew how it would be. Everyone else would already know each other, and by the end of the day, I'd be one of the leftovers. I'd make friends with another leftover, but it wasn't the same as a real friend. Leftovers were like Velcro—you were stuck together. With a real friend, it was like a zipper—you fit together.

Andrew had it easier because he was good at sports. He could go up to a crowd of boys at recess and say, "I can pitch seventy miles an hour," and have instant friends.

That day I'd felt sick to my stomach with nerves. Mrs. Denton, the teacher, asked us to stand in a circle and share something we knew. I stood next to a biggish girl with blond hair, blue eyes, and a round face. It was Lori, only I didn't know it yet.

When it was my turn, I said I had a telescope, and I knew all about the stars. I said the earth spins around like a top that never slows down. Mrs. Denton looked so impressed, I started to spin like I was in orbit. I spun three times before everything in my stomach orbited right up my throat and all over Lori's sandals. It turned

out I didn't have a case of nerves. I had a case of stomach flu. I stayed home for two days.

On the second afternoon, my mom made me go to Lori's house. I stood on the front step, and when she came to the door, I gave her a new pair of pink sandals my mom had bought.

"Sorry," I said. "I didn't know I was sick."

She turned the shoes over in her hands. "It's okay," she said. "Mrs. Denton let us spend the whole morning in recess while they washed the carpet."

She rubbed a finger over a white plastic flower on the buckle. "Do you have a dog or a cat?"

I shook my head. "I had a hamster once."

Her eyes brightened. "Me, too," she said. "Mine died."

I gasped. "So did mine!"

For a second, we just smiled at each other. Then she said, "There's an empty seat next to me at school. If you want."

I said that sounded okay. But it was better than okay.

That day reminded me of flying with my dad and getting to sit in the cockpit. You look out the window, but it's just tons of clouds—thick clouds everywhere so you feel like you could get lost inside them and never find your way out. But then, there's this instant when the nose of the plane breaks through the clouds, and the world is suddenly full of sun.

That's how it felt, standing on Lori's front porch. Like the sun had just come out.

Ever since that day, Lori had been my best friend. It was like we were family—better than family. Because while stuff at home was falling apart, Lori was always there.

We climbed back into bed, and I stretched out beneath the cool sheets. "'Night," I said.

"'Nigh," she said, the end of the word getting swallowed up in a yawn.

Then it got quiet so all I could hear was the sound of us breathing. I had this trick where I tried to match my breath with Lori's so it sounded like we were one person. It always relaxed me so I could fall asleep.

I was just on the edge of a dream when I heard Lori murmur softly, as if to herself, "Level One, but serious potential for Level Two."

It took me a long time to fall asleep after that.

♪ 5 ♫

Five more minutes. I watched the clock over the band room door, my heart keeping tempo with the second hand. Not much longer now.

It was Monday afternoon, and nearly time for rehearsal to start. Aaron sat next to me, pretending to wet his reed. I did the same thing, even though my reed was already as soggy as an old bowl of Cheerios. But with our reeds in our mouths, we could secretly talk trash about whoever we wanted.

Like Michael Malone.

He stood at the podium talking to Mr. Wayne. Neither of us knew how his audition had gone today or where he'd be sitting. But we'd know in a minute.

If he'd get his butt moving.

I leaned right as Frank lumbered up the risers, banging his clarinet case on a chair. I winced at the noise. It was already loud enough in the room to make my ears cry. Kevin Marks, a trumpet player, had decided to do duck calls with his mouthpiece, and Tanner was playing "Chopsticks" on the xylophone. Everyone else was either talking or warming up their instruments. Something flew past my face, but I didn't take my eyes off Michael to look. Probably one of José's drumsticks.

"Is he in any of your classes?" Aaron asked from behind the screen of his reed.

"Nope," I said. "He's not in any of Lori's classes, either, but we saw him at lunch."

"How did that go?"

I knew Aaron hadn't been in the cafeteria today—he spent Monday lunches in computer lab with the Science Olympiad team. "Okay."

"You sound disappointed."

I shrugged, but Aaron was right. Secretly, I'd envisioned Michael acting like a complete loser in front of a crowd—including Lori. But he'd walked into the cafeteria with a brown-bag lunch, stopped to say hi to Kerry and Misa, then gone to sit with Brandon and the other guys from band.

I flipped the reed over. "Alesia made her move, as expected."

"And?"

"She swung her hips—and struck out." I sighed, a little bummed out about that, too. Michael had ignored Alesia and her hips while he talked to Brandon. And Lori had seen the whole thing.

"He's so hot, isn't he?" Lori had whispered.

After that, I'd spent the rest of the time watching Michael out of the corner of my eye—hoping to catch him with a straw up his nose or jelly stuck to his chin. But when I accidentally caught his eye, he gave me a nod back. A friendly kind of nod.

It was hard to hate someone who smiled at you from across the cafeteria. But at least I was right about his lips. They *were* pouty.

"Is he going to talk to Mr. Wayne for the whole practice?" I grumbled.

Aaron shrugged and bent down to his case. He lifted a pack of Sudoku puzzles and set it on our music stand. Aaron and I had shared a stand since the end of last year. I figured this year he'd move up a row—he was every bit as good as Angie, who sat first chair, and he played way better than I did. But Aaron must suck at auditions because here he was sitting in the second row again. I'm not sure when the Sudoku puzzles had started, but now we did one during most practices. From Mr. Wayne's spot on the podium, it looked like we were marking the music. Really, we took turns filling in the squares whenever Mr. Wayne stopped to work with the other sections. Numbers were one thing I was good at, but Aaron was better than me. He could fill out a Sudoku, keep up with the music, and calculate how many more minutes of practice, all at the same time.

"Three-star or four-star?" Aaron asked, holding the puzzles.

"Let's go easy—make it a two-star," I said. Then a flash of movement at the podium caught my eye. *Michael.*

My heart jumped, and I bit down on my reed, shredding the tip. "Snap," I muttered.

Aaron straightened the music that didn't need straightening. Michael had grabbed a folding chair and was headed our way.

I dumped the broken reed in my case and reached for a new one. I pretended to study the different reeds while I stopped breathing and waited to see where Michael ended up with that chair.

If he sat in the front row with Angie and Brooke, that meant he was better. But if he sat behind me in the third row with Melanie, Jamie, and Frank, that meant I was better.

He stopped at the front row and my heart paused midbeat. Then he shrugged at Angie and Brooke, and climbed up one level. To my level. *To me.*

"Looks like I'm playing second part, next to you."

Next to me?

"In front?" I asked, my voice croaking. "Or behind?"

His fingers tightened around the chair. "Behind."

Yes!

My heart kicked back into action, pumping with joy. *Mr. Wayne put me first.* I scooted my chair closer to Aaron, and we swapped smiles. *I'm better than Youth Symphony boy! It's going to be okay—I'll make Honor Band and—*

Then Michael's chair bumped mine as he unfolded it. Reality hit. *I'm not better by much.* I swallowed. *What if I'm not better at all? Maybe it is a tie, and Mr. Wayne put me first because I've been here longer.*

By now, everyone had begun warm-ups. I snuck a glance at Lori, and she flashed me a thumbs-up. That made me feel a little better. I straightened my reed, then tightened the ligature to keep it from shifting on the mouthpiece. My heart still beat too fast, and I took a deep breath. Something smelled like apple— Michael's shampoo? I shifted in my chair. Could he smell me? Did I smell like tacos from lunch?

I rippled through the low notes, but I had my ears tuned for Michael. He ran his fingers over the keys—his nails were short and bitten-down so the edges were a little red. The keys clacked as he played through a chromatic scale. He tapped his foot and one ragged black shoelace skated onto my sneaker. I moved my foot away, wondering if he'd at least tie his dress shoes for concerts.

"I've got to share your music today," Michael said. "Coach says he'll get me my own for tomorrow. Guess the copier was down."

"Yeah, it usually is," I said. I gave Aaron a look, then slid the music stand so it was more in front of me.

Aaron picked up the Sudoku and dropped it back in his case.

"You do puzzles during practice?" Michael asked.

"Sort of," I said.

"It's cool by me. Not everyone is into band."

"I'm into band," I said quickly.

He shrugged, but I could tell it was one of those "yeah, right" shrugs. My shoulders tensed, and so did every other muscle right down to my fingertips. I looked back over at Lori—as if she'd be able to sense his jerkness from across the room—but she was focused on her music.

Then Mr. Wayne tapped his baton on the podium and called for Angie to give everyone a tuning note. She played a C, and we all joined in. Michael pulled his barrel out, then eased it back in a millimeter as if he had a perfect ear for tuning. Unlike me. I pulled my barrel out, too, but I was never exactly sure. Aaron would tell me if I was off.

Mr. Wayne tapped his podium again and everyone quieted. "Before we get started on the music," he said, "I'd like you to welcome our newest member." He gestured to Michael. "Michael Malone has joined us from Texas. I hope you'll all make him feel at home."

Or could we just make him go home?

"Now," Mr. Wayne said, clearing his throat. "I know you're all looking forward to Band Night Out. We'll be staying at the Sunfire Hotel after your auditions, two weeks from Saturday. But if you don't pay, you can't play. That means fund-raisers."

A chorus of groans filled the room.

"Remember, we're in the final push. We have events scheduled each and every weekend. Make sure you participate." Mr. Wayne scowled in a wide circle. "However, let's not lose sight of the main purpose of the day: District Honor Band auditions."

Another even louder round of groans rose up like surround sound.

"I don't need to tell you how important it is that you do well. This is a major part of your grade, as well as your opportunity to make the band."

Brooke raised her clarinet from the front row and wiggled it to get Mr. Wayne's attention. "What if we're going to be gone the weekend of District Honor Band?"

"I'm aware of your plans, Brooke, but you'll still need to audition for your grade. It's a requirement for everyone. You should have all completed the sign-up sheet marking whether you're performing a solo or a duet and the name of the piece," Mr. Wayne added.

I swapped a nod with Lori. She'd signed us up for our duet the first day.

Mr. Wayne paused a second, then pointed to Michael. "That reminds me, Mr. Malone. You'll need to find an audition piece if you don't already have one. Let me know if you need help."

"Thanks, Coach."

Mr. Wayne beamed.

Suck-up.

Mr. Wayne went on. "Check the schedule on my door

for your practices with me. Each of you will be assigned two sessions—a first run-through and a final dress rehearsal. If you require additional help, see me after class."

He tapped the podium again. "Now, to the music. 'Air for Band'!"

Michael leaned forward, and his knee bumped mine. "Ow," I muttered.

"Sorry. Can you move over?" he asked.

I shifted my seat and rubbed my left leg. Lori thought he had nice knees? Maybe if you liked hairy boulders.

Mr. Wayne raised the baton, and I took a fluttery breath. At least we were starting with my favorite piece. The clarinets had the melody, and the notes were easy enough that I could relax and let the sound flow. I pushed my shoulders back and blew from down deep, letting air fill the clarinet—and the music fill me. During the last few months, things had started to click, and there were times when I heard myself play and it sounded almost . . . beautiful. Times when my clarinet felt like a part of me. When I thought maybe I could hear a future in the music I made. If only I could make those times stretch and last.

By the end of the piece, I could tell Michael had fast fingers and he sight-read better than I could. He'd never seen the music before, but he played almost every note. A fresh wave of worry hit me, taking my confidence with it.

Aaron switched out the music to a Sousa march and gave me a smile as if he could tell. Maybe he could—I felt sort of shaky.

Finally, Mr. Wayne glanced at the clock, then lay down his baton. "That's it for today. Nice work." Everyone started packing up.

"So Brandon filled me in on Band Night Out," Michael said, flipping open his case. "An overnight at a hotel—nice!"

"Yeah," I said, "that part will be fun."

"Not the audition?"

"Not unless you like standing in front of a firing squad."

"That good, huh?"

I loosened my ligature. "We audition for Dr. Hallady. He's a scary guy."

Michael slid his reed into its plastic holder. "Then it's a good thing I don't scare easy."

"Yeah, well." I rolled my eyes. "For a guy who's been in a *youth symphony,* what's one more audition?"

"Right." Then he laughed—only it wasn't a confident *ha-ha* kind of laugh like I expected. I shot him a look, but he turned away.

"What does that mean?" I asked.

He shrugged and fitted his bell into the case. "Nothing."

"It didn't sound like—" I paused, distracted, as he pulled off the bottom section of his clarinet and set it next to the bell. I couldn't help but point. "Aren't you going to swab it out?"

He pulled off the middle piece. "Nah."

"But it's dripping spit."

"It's just water."

"Spit is not water. It's full of digestive enzymes."

He blinked at me. "Digestive *enzymes*?"

I turned away, my cheeks burning. "Forget it." I pulled out my own swab—a handkerchief with a string attached. I worked it through the inside of each section. So much for trying to be nice to him. If he wanted a saliva-infested clarinet . . .

"So Lor said you guys are playing a duet."

I turned back toward him, my mouth a little open. *"Lor?"*

Michael snapped his case shut. "You're lucky she's your partner. I'll bet she's good."

"She's the best," I said. "And she hates *Lor*."

"Yeah?"

"Yeah."

His eyes shone as he looked toward her seat. "Maybe it depends on who says it."

I fought the urge to whack his arm with part of my clarinet—I'd just dent my keys.

"So," he said, "if only three clarinetists from Dakota can make District Honor Band . . ." His voice trailed off as he looked around at the other players. "Sounds like Brooke won't be there. That leaves Angie and Aaron ahead of me." He paused, then added, "And you."

I fitted my mouthpiece in the case and closed it. "Yeah. And me."

"I guess that makes you the competition."

"I guess so." I met his gaze straight on. His eyes were nice—green with bits of yellow like colored glass. Nice eyes that sent worry crackling through me like a live wire. As he stepped off the riser, I looked for Lori, panic rushing through me. She looked back, smiling.

Smiling?

Then I realized she wasn't smiling at me. She was smiling at Michael.

I lay on the floor of my room. It was still Monday but only for two more hours. I yawned, but I didn't want to get in bed. From the floor, I could see the stars and a moonless sky out my window.

The phone was still warm in my hands. Lori and I had finally hung up after way too long, when I should have been working on my science handout. We would start dissecting next week, and Mr. Howard had sent home a whole packet of worksheets.

But I'd just wanted to talk to Lori. As if nothing was different. As if nothing was happening to make things different. I'd felt so weird after band. Nervous. Unsettled. And being on the phone with Lori tonight had helped.

For a while.

We covered school, Band Night Out, and what we were going to do at the hotel. We talked about the movies coming out and whether Johnny Depp was too old to be hot and what movie character we'd want for our first kiss. I said Will Turner from *Pirates*, and Lori said Jacob from *Twilight*. Then she said Michael kind of looked like Jacob, except his hair was lighter and curlier. And suddenly, it was all different. Instead of the two of us, it was like Michael was on the phone, also.

I could tell she was picturing him in her head and so was I, but I knew we weren't picturing anything alike. It made Lori feel farther away, no matter how tightly I gripped the phone.

And when we were just about to hang up, her voice grew soft. "I know you're worried about band stuff, but I don't want you to hate him, Tay," she said. "I want you to like him."

Because I do. She didn't say it, but that's what she meant.

So now I lay on the carpet, wishing on the stars.

When I was little, I thought stars were streetlights God had put out for pilots like my dad when he had night flights. I'd wait for the stars to come out and know that wherever Dad was, he'd see them, too. And he'd find his way home in the dark.

Dad had bought me my first book on astronomy. I still had it. According to the book, stars were really balls of hot gas, constantly spinning in motion. But from my window, they didn't look like they were doing anything but twinkling. You could always count on the stars to be there, same as the night before.

That's how I wanted things to stay. Exactly the same.

I ran my fingers through the scratchy fibers of carpet, holding tight. Maybe it wasn't fair to blame Michael Malone, but his moving here was ruining everything. Because of him, I might not make District Honor Band. Worse, he was trying to steal away my best friend.

How could Lori, who had never liked a guy before, suddenly like *him*? It couldn't be for real. Even if she did fall under his bony-kneed spell, it wasn't like it would change anything. Not really. Not between us.

Even if you *like-liked* a guy, how could that take the place of a best friend?

♩ 6 ♫

"Why do you always get stuck doing this stuff?" I asked Mom. "Can't the other teachers staple packets?"

She handed me a stack of papers. "I didn't get stuck. I volunteered."

"Well, then why do *I* always get stuck doing this stuff?"

She smiled. "Because you're a wonderful daughter."

I sighed and slid a GROW YOUR GARDEN coloring packet into the electric stapler. *Bam*, the staple shot through the pages, and I set the packet on top of the finished pile. I wasn't being wonderful on purpose. This wasn't how I wanted to spend my Thursday night, but I'd finished my homework, spent nearly an hour going over the evil thirty-second notes in my duet, and now it was either staple packets or worry. "How many of these do you have to do?"

"One hundred," she said, gesturing to a box at her feet. "But most of them are already done." She stuck a white cover on top of the yellow and blue pages she'd spread out on the kitchen island. "I can finish up myself."

I shrugged and watched another staple shoot into the pages. "I guess I can do a few more."

The kitchen felt warm from the oven. It smelled good—like the chicken and garlic potatoes we'd had for dinner. Andrew had baseball practice, so he'd eaten earlier. Now that he was sixteen, he borrowed Mom's car and drove himself. That meant a lot of nights when it was just Mom and me. She'd started talking more at dinner, as if she could fill up the empty chairs with her voice.

In the two months since the separation, it was like she'd tried to wipe away all the signs that Dad had ever lived here. She'd taken his place mat off the table, so now there were three spots instead of four. And Dad's coffee mug was up in the cupboard instead of on the draining board, and the hat he kept on a hook by the back door was gone. Things were just . . . gone . . . and with nothing to replace them, it felt like there were holes everywhere. Holes in our house. Holes in our family. Even holes in my mom.

"Isn't Lori coming over tonight?" she asked. "I thought you were going to practice together."

I held out my hand for another packet. "I thought so,

too, but she had to go to some music program for her sister."

"I heard you practicing before dinner. It's coming along."

"Not fast enough." I had tried practicing standing up in case that helped, but I couldn't hold my clarinet steady. Nothing felt right tonight—my tone seemed fuzzy, my rhythm was off, and I still couldn't get through the fast parts without tripping over my fingers. "It sounds stupid when it's just me."

"It's not supposed to sound perfect on your own. It's a duet," Mom said.

"But I don't do the melody right without Lori."

"I'm sure you'll work it out with a little more practice. You don't give yourself enough credit."

I rolled my eyes. "You're such a mom."

"I think I've just been insulted," she said, smiling. She handed me another packet. "You and Lori did a duet last year, and you pulled it off. You'll do the same this year."

"Nothing's the same this year," I said.

"Such as?"

A pair of green-yellow eyes popped into my head. I shoved the packet in the stapler so hard, it double-stapled.

Mom's eyebrows rose an inch. When her eyes weren't all red, puffy, and tired, they were pretty—dark brown and shaped like half-moons.

"It's just the new guy. Michael Malone."

"The one who sits next to you?"

I nodded and leaned on the counter, watching her stack the pages, but not really seeing anything except Michael. "He doesn't say anything during practice, but I can tell he's listening, waiting for me to mess up. So he can say he's better."

"Is he?"

"No," I said. Then I shrugged. "I don't know. Maybe. He never squeaks, not even on the high notes."

"You don't squeak, either."

"Yeah, I do—when I get nervous. And I can't help getting nervous with him sitting next to me."

"Then ignore him."

"It's not that easy." I flicked a nail through the corner of a packet, fanning the pages like a deck of cards. "He's always there. If he's not staring at me, he's staring at Lori."

"Lori?"

"He's got these beady eyes. You don't notice it at first, but they're too close together, like a gorilla or something."

"A beady-eyed gorilla?" She handed me another packet.

I nodded as I fed it to the stapler. "And his knees are bony, and he never ties his shoes. The laces are always trailing in the dirt, and I mean, who knows what germs he's dragging around with him. Plus, he never swabs out his clarinet."

"What does Lori think of him?"

I shrugged. "She likes him, I guess. When he gets out of school, he wants to play in his father's band in New York, so she thinks that's cool."

Mom made this noise in the back of her throat that was supposed to be understanding but was actually annoying. "You just need to concentrate on your own playing."

"I am. I just wish Lori had more time. Our first read-through for Mr. Wayne is on Monday."

"You've got the whole weekend," she said, sliding the last pages together.

A gray piece of construction paper fluttered off the counter. I grabbed it in midair and turned it over.

"Auditions for community theater?" I scanned the flyer, then shot my mom a horrified look. "No way am I doing this."

She snatched the flyer out of my hands. "It's not for you. It's for me."

I gasped. "You?"

She set the flyer back on the counter. "Mrs. Lansing gave it to me. Something I might want to get involved in."

"Community theater?" I puckered around the words as if I were saying "toe fungus" or "chronic canker sore."

"Yes, community theater," she said sharply. "Auditions are tomorrow night, and I'm going. You'll be at your father's."

I rolled my eyes. "Fine. But why can't I stay here? I hate going to that house. It's always so dark, and I'm afraid to touch anything or I'll leave fingerprints."

"Tatum," she said, and her voice sounded really tired all of a sudden. "It's just very clean because your dad is rarely in town. He feels bad that you don't spend more time there."

"Well, I feel bad that he doesn't come home."

She sighed—but it was one of those heavy breaths full of stuff she didn't have to say because I'd already heard it before.

We need some time.

Even adults don't always have the answers.

We're doing our best.

It's not about you; it's about us.

Ha. It sure felt like it was about me.

"Anyway," she said, "you'll be there while I'm at the audition."

I pulled the flyer closer with the edge of one finger and read the description.

Harry and the Heiress:
An Assisted-Living Love Story
By local playwright Anita Weebans
Desert Rose Nursing Home

"A romance with old people?" I asked. "I don't get why you'd want to do something like this." Once, Mom had dragged me to a musical her friend Mrs. Lansing was in. It was a bunch of white-hairs singing off-key in a church auditorium.

"Because it might be fun," she said.

Fun? Was she really that desperate? I rubbed a hand over my stomach where garlic potatoes suddenly churned. Of course she was that desperate. She sat at home and watched tearjerkers and ate Junior Mints. And I'd overheard her talking to Grandma about how awkward it was to go out with her friends because they all still had husbands. She didn't need community theater. She needed Dad back.

So what if his new job kept him away so much? Having Dad a little bit was better than not having him at all.

Why was I the only one who could see that?

I looked up from my sheet music at the sound of the front door slamming. My bedroom clock glowed 8:54 p.m.—Andrew must be home. My fingers stilled on the keys of my clarinet. I didn't have my mouthpiece attached—I'd just been slowly going over the hard section of the duet, working my fingers over the keys. If I did it enough times, they would learn what to do without my brain having to tell them. At least I hoped so. I started the thirty-second notes again, but mostly I listened.

There was a soft muffle of voices—Mom saying hi and asking about practice—and then Andrew's size 11 shoes on the stairs. He pounded up them, three or four at a time, and the floor shook a little as he reached the top. The upstairs was just big enough for a computer desk at the top of the landing, and our two rooms connected by the bathroom.

Then I heard Andrew's bedroom door, a slight squeak as it closed. A thud and then another thud—him kicking his shoes off. Silence. He'd be leaning over his iPod right now, turning it on and . . . a drumbeat thrummed from his room as the music kicked on. I smiled a little—I could time his movements to the second.

A sudden sting of tears filled my eyes, which was *so stupid.* Getting drippy over my brother and his routine—*please.* I should be glad when Andrew was playing baseball or staying over at Dad's—it meant I got the whole upstairs to myself. But I liked the squeaks and the thuds. I liked him being home . . . *our* home. I set down my clarinet and slid out of bed. I opened up my side of the bathroom and walked through.

"Andrew?" I knocked on his door.

"Yeah?"

I swung it open and leaned against the frame, trying not to breathe in the combo of manly musk and sweaty cleats. A dirty baseball jersey lay on the floor next to muddy socks and his Adobe Wildcats baseball hat. Andrew sat on his mattress, phone in his hand. He'd grown so much the past year, Mom kept promising to buy him a bigger bed.

He rubbed his fingers through his hair, scratching along the indent from his baseball hat. "What do you want?"

"Nothing." I pushed the door out with a foot and pulled it back in with my hand, listening to it *whoosh* as it swept across the carpet. "Did Mom tell you she's trying out for a play?"

He looked up from his phone. "What kind of play?"

"A lame one."

"Do we have to go watch her?"

"I don't know. She hasn't tried out yet. Auditions are tomorrow, and she wants me to go to Dad's." I swung the door out and in again. "I hate that house."

He typed something in his phone. "Yeah, it's dark."

"And . . . shiny. Is it weird being there at night?"

He hit a key on his phone and set it down. Then he pulled up a leg and rested one arm over his knee. "No, it's just . . . quiet. Mom's always got the dishwasher running or the laundry going. Over at Dad's it's nothingness."

"I'm not going to sleep there."

"No one said you have to."

"I don't know why you do it."

He shrugged. "It's still Dad."

"But it's not our house," I said. "Just because he moves, I'm supposed to act like it's my house? Like we all belong there?" I pushed at the door again. "Has he said anything? About Mom or coming home?"

Andrew shook his head. "He asks how we're doing."

"What do you say?"

"We're fine."

I straightened. "You shouldn't say that. We're not."

He gave me a long look. "I'm not saying it doesn't suck. But we *are* fine." Then he ran his hand over his chin, back and forth, as if he were brushing off crumbs.

I frowned. "What are you doing?"

"Nothing."

I rolled my eyes. "Well, anyway, we're not fine. We're messed up. Dad's flying off to China, and Mom's going to be acting in nursing homes."

He rubbed a finger over his face again. I squinted as something dark caught the light. "Is that a hair on your chin?"

Andrew grinned. "Yeah."

I moved in closer, climbing over a pile of clothes to see better. One dark hair poked out of the bottom of his smooth chin. For the past few months, Andrew had sprouted the beginnings of a fuzzy blond mustache, but this was a dark, actually legit, hair.

"Pull that out," I said. "It's weird."

"It's my beard."

"It's a hair!"

"It's a beast of a hair!" He pushed off the bed and

went to stand in front of his closet mirror. He tilted his head and studied his chin. "It's good luck. Since it's been growing, the baseball team hasn't lost a game."

"You lost last week," I said.

"But we won this week."

"Because of that hair?"

His grin widened. "Fear the beard, baby."

I blew out a breath. "What does Emily think?"

"I don't know."

"She's going to hate it."

"So she'll hate it." He shot me a look. "You gotta stop worrying about what other people think, Tay. Grow a backbone."

I pretended the words didn't sting. "If I grow a backbone as raggedy as that beard, we really are going to be a messed-up family."

He laughed, and his eyes, so much like Mom's, softened. Andrew had grown tall and lean like Dad, but he had Mom's almond-shaped brown eyes. I got Mom's round face and ski-slope nose, but Dad's olive-green eyes. We were both pieces of them . . . and we were ourselves because they'd made us together. Because they were together. Now it was all coming apart. Like strands of DNA unraveling.

"I don't want them to split up, Andrew," I said.

He shrugged. "I know."

"So what do we do?"

"I don't think there's anything we can do. They messed it up; they have to fix it."

"What if they don't? What happens to our family?"

He sighed. "I guess we'll be the way we are now."

"Yeah," I said. "That's what I'm worried about."

♪ 7 ♫

Are you sure she's coming?" Mr. Wayne asked me. "Maybe she forgot."

"I reminded her," I said. "I know she knows." I paced back to his office door and looked down the hall. Nothing but emptiness and the odd smell of plastic sweat that seemed to lurk around the band room.

"It's not like Lori to be late," Mr. Wayne added.

Yeah, I wanted to say. *It's also not like Lori to be busy for practically the whole weekend.* Sure, we'd done a *Pirates* marathon on Saturday, but she'd spent almost the whole time on her phone sending texts. To guess who. Finally, I'd told her to stop or she'd end up crippled with finger strain.

She'd barely paused in her typing. "I think it's helping my dexterity."

Great. So now beady-eyed, bony-kneed Michael was helping her with dexterity. What a guy.

On Sunday, she'd gone to her grandma's house and then couldn't practice at night because she was behind on math homework. Which she wouldn't have been except that she'd wasted so much time texting Michael.

But this was different. This was our first time playing our duet for Mr. Wayne. This was District Honor Band, and my grade, and me chewing holes out of the inside of my cheek.

Why didn't she answer her phone? I stared at my cell as if I could will it to ring. The dark screen stared back.

Mr. Wayne shuffled some papers on his desk. "We don't have much time before students begin arriving."

"Can we wait a few more minutes?" I asked. "Please."

His eyes smiled at me. "Why don't you have a seat, Tatum? Let's use the time to have a little chat."

"A chat?" I said hesitantly, but I walked back in and sat down. I'd already set up everything—two chairs and a music stand for our play-through. I'd put my clarinet together, and it was resting on my case. "About what?"

Mr. Wayne took a sip of his coffee, then stretched back. The chair creaked as it tilted. "I wondered if you've considered performing a solo. It's not too late."

"Me? A solo?" I shook my head so hard that my ponytail whipped across my ear. "No way."

"This will be the third year you've performed a duet. I think it would be good for you to stretch yourself."

"I wouldn't stretch, Mr. Wayne. I'd explode."

His fingers tapped a rhythm on his desk. "You've

greatly improved this year, Tatum. Surely you recognize that?"

I thought back to the other day. To times when I could feel the music. When my lungs opened up and it all came flowing out. But I could never play like that for a judge. "I'd be too nervous," I told Mr. Wayne.

"I could help you choose a piece you'd feel comfortable with. One that plays to your strengths."

"What do you mean, my strengths?" I chewed at my cheek again.

"Let's try an experiment, shall we?"

I looked at the door. *Where is Lori?*

"Don't panic," Mr. Wayne said, a smile edging the corners of his mouth. "I just want you to play the first line of your duet."

I reached for my clarinet and licked the reed. "Just the first line?"

"Concentrate on a full sound." He leaned forward. "Nice and slow."

I took a breath and started to play, but only got through three measures before I stopped. "I sound like a beached whale."

"Nonsense," he said. "You have a very nice tone."

"But I sounded so spitty."

"Yes, you did." He rose from his chair and sat next to me. "Hand me your clarinet."

He took it, unscrewed the ligature, and handed me the reed. "Wet this again."

While I did, he studied the duet.

"This is a very challenging piece, Tatum. It's quite technical in places."

"Lori thought it would make a good impression with the judge."

"It might," he said, "if you excelled at technical passages."

I handed the wet reed back to him, and he set it on the mouthpiece, which was pretty gross considering it was covered in my spit. But he didn't seem to notice as he talked.

"Your reed was just a little low. Be sure it's correctly placed. You'll know when you're getting a nice sound." He pointed to the sheet music. "Now, let's look at this section with the thirty-second notes."

"I'm working on those."

"Instead of playing all the notes, just play the first note of each beat. Give me quarter notes, long and full."

I slid the mouthpiece between my lips and took a breath. A low full B hummed through the bell and filled the office. I finished the two lines and then looked at him.

He grinned so wide his eyes were just slivers of brown. "That was marvelous, Tatum. Lovely."

"It's a lot easier than playing all those notes," I said, laughing a little. It had sounded good. Really good.

"Obviously, you need to work on your technical skills and improve. And you will in time. However," he added, "you truly shine in areas of musical expression and the tone you produce. I don't think this duet serves you well. Not as well as the right solo."

"But—"

He held up a hand. "I know you feel more comfortable with Lori, and I know that worked well for you last year. But this year is different. There's more at stake."

I curled my fingers over the clarinet. "You mean more than District Honor Band?"

"Yes." He sighed with his mouth closed so the air whistled out his nose. "We'll get to that in a minute. First, District Honor Band. You know only three clarinet players from our school will make it."

"Believe me, I know," I said. "But Brooke is gone the weekend of the concert like last year. That leaves Angie and Aaron and they're both amazing, so they'll make it." I took a breath. "Melanie, Jamie, and Frank all play third part, and I think I can beat them." I rubbed my hand along the barrel. "Which leaves Michael. You think he's better than I am?"

"That's for the judge to determine," Mr. Wayne said gently. "But I will say that you're both at a similar level. It might be very close."

Acid bubbled up in my stomach. "In other words, I need all the help I can get."

"He might be thinking the same thing—that he needs all the help he can get." Mr. Wayne gave me a pointed look. "Regardless, those who perform a solo are rewarded with more points. It won't affect Lori because she's also performing a solo for her own audition. But it will affect you."

"I still think a duet is my best chance."

He sighed. "You realize Dr. Hallady will judge your performance this year?"

I gulped, picturing the band director from Adobe High in my head. "I know. I'm already having nightmares about it."

Mr. Wayne smiled. "He's not as scary as he looks. But he will use these auditions as an opportunity to evaluate incoming students. Yes, there will be another chance to audition for the regular band, but a strong performance now could very well earn you a spot in his Wind Ensemble next year."

"But that's the top band at Adobe!"

"Don't you want to be in Wind Ensemble?"

"I didn't think I had a chance," I admitted.

"Wind Ensemble is not out of your range. If it's something you wanted to do, I could help you."

"You don't really think—"

"I certainly do think." He reached for the duet and studied it, shaking his head just a little. "The first step would be to prepare a solo."

"I'm not sure," I said, but a shivery feeling worked its way through me. *Mr. Wayne thinks I have a chance at Wind Ensemble?*

"Will you promise me you'll think about it?"

I nodded.

"Good enough." He set the music back on the stand. "We really can't wait a moment longer. Why don't we get started?"

Started? "But I can't do a duet by myself."

He folded his hands over his middle. "We'll just concentrate on your part."

My stomach clenched, suddenly nervous again. Something really terrible must have happened to keep Lori away.

I slid to the edge of my chair, goose bumps rising where the cold metal touched my legs. I focused on the music, counted out the beat in my head, took a breath, and began.

And missed a flat. I screwed up my face at the awful sound. "Sorry, Mr. Wayne."

I started again, but now my heart raced and I couldn't keep the beat straight in my head. After a muffled trill and another dropped flat, I gave up, fighting the urge to whack my head against the music stand.

"Relax," Mr. Wayne said gently.

Why do people always say that, as if it's something you can do on command? I set my fingers over the keys—even they felt cold now. Or was it my fingers? I shivered and rested the bell of my clarinet between my knees to keep it from shaking. Only, my knees shook, too.

I bet he was sorry he'd ever said anything about Wind Ensemble. Me do a solo? *Ha!*

Suddenly, the door flew open and Lori rushed in. "Sorry," she gasped, out of breath. "I'm really sorry!"

I was so happy to see her that tears welled up in my eyes. "Are you okay? I called and called, but you didn't answer your phone."

"I forgot to charge it last night." She dumped her backpack on the floor and set her flute case on Mr. Wayne's desk. "The battery died this morning."

"Where were you?" I asked.

"We about gave up on you," Mr. Wayne added.

"I know. I'm really sorry." She flipped the lid of her case and had the pieces together in the time it took Mr. Wayne to cross back to his desk chair.

Her eyes locked with mine. "I am so, so sorry!"

"I thought you were dead or something."

Though she didn't look dead—or even all that upset as she slid into the chair next to me. She looked really good in a blue V-neck and jean shorts—were they new? Had she dropped another size? I suddenly felt lame in a faded pink T-shirt and jeans.

She blew a few warm-up notes. "You ready?"

I nodded.

She played a note for tuning and I joined in.

"Pull out," she whispered. "Just a little."

I adjusted my barrel, and we blew another note. *I can't even tune myself—what am I thinking?*

Lori glanced at Mr. Wayne. "Okay, we're ready."

She used her flute to mark the beat. *One, two, three* . . .

I followed along, my fingers a lot less wobbly with her next to me. Two lines in, I got into the rhythm of the piece and made it through without too many errors. Well, except for the thirty-second notes.

Lori circled the end of her flute, my signal to stop, and the last note faded into silence. We both let out a breath. I sagged back in my seat.

"Nice beginning," Mr. Wayne said, as the warning bell sounded for first period. He ripped a piece of paper off his notebook. "We don't have time to go over my notes right now, but you can read them on your own."

I reached around the music stand and took it. There were half a dozen scrawls in Mr. Wayne's messy writing.

"Miss Van Sant, you have a solo read-through with me today at lunch, correct?"

"I'll be there."

"See that you're on time. And, Miss Austin?"

I snapped my case shut and looked up. "Please think about what we discussed."

I nodded, but it was a lie. Who was I kidding? I couldn't play without Lori. After this morning, I was sure of it.

If only I was sure of her.

◎◎

"What did he mean?" Lori asked as soon as we closed the office door behind us.

The hall was crammed now, and I had to dodge a group of kids heading to morning choir. After Mr. Wayne's soundproof office, it felt like someone had turned up the volume on the world.

"I'll tell you later," I said, raising my voice enough to be heard. "So what happened? Where were you?"

"Hey, Tay-Lo!" someone shouted. "Wait up."

Only Misa had a voice so high-pitched it carried over everyone else's. We both turned and, sure enough, there were Misa and Kerry at the end of the hall.

While we waited, Lori grabbed my arm. "Remember when you made me promise that you'd be the first to know when I got kissed?"

My heart screeched to a halt.

"Well." She beamed. "You're the first."

Before I could breathe again, Kerry and Misa caught up.

"What's going on?" Kerry asked.

Lori grinned, her cheeks neon red. "It's official," she said. "Michael and I are dating."

♪ 8 ♫

Oh. My. God." Kerry's dark eyes widened with each word.

"You are sooooo lucky!" Misa said.

They went on and on all the way to English, which was good, because if I opened my mouth I was afraid of what might come out.

I thought you were dead under a bus, and you were kissing Michael Malone? You were sucking face with Pouty Lips?

We got to language arts with time to spare. Mrs. Law sat behind her desk, thumbing through our literature book. She never bothered to look up until the bell rang, and then she'd blink at us, surprised, as if she didn't know where we'd all come from.

I didn't like English as much as science, but this was still my favorite class because all four of us had it together. Misa and I sat in the front row, and Kerry and

Lori sat behind us. We dropped our packs, slid into our seats, and leaned in to talk. I crossed my arms over my chest, my stomach as tightly clenched as my hands.

"You and Michael Malone," Misa said, for about the tenth time.

"I could tell from that day at the car wash," Kerry said.

Misa gathered her red hair in one hand and fanned herself with it. "He's completely hot."

"I know." Lori grinned and nodded like a bobblehead.

"So when did it happen?" Misa asked.

"This morning," she said. "I was supposed to meet Tay for a play-through. I completely forgot."

"You forgot a band thing?" Kerry gasped. "This must be love."

"Did you know?" Misa asked me.

I shook my head. "I thought something awful must have happened."

"I felt terrible," Lori said, beaming.

"Details, details," Kerry demanded, wiggling her fingers.

"Well," Lori said, "we were texting last night, and I said I had to go to school early. He said he'd meet me by the tennis courts. So we met, and then he asked me."

Kerry nudged my foot with her flip-flop. "You don't look too thrilled, Tay."

"Because I got stuck in Mr. Wayne's office all by myself."

"It's not like I planned it," Lori said.

"Well, maybe he did."

"What?" Lori shot me a surprised look. "What does that mean?"

I hadn't thought it out, but as I spoke, it started to make sense. "Maybe he planned it that way to screw up our play-through."

"He wouldn't do that!" Then she aimed a double eye-roll at Kerry and Misa. "Tay doesn't like Michael."

I grabbed the edge of my desk. "I didn't say I don't like him. I'm just worried about our duet."

"You still have plenty of time to practice," Misa said.

"Yeah," Kerry added. "They can't kiss *all* day."

"But they can trrr*yyyy*," Misa sang.

"You guys!" Lori hissed, but then she giggled.

"Maybe you can work on your embouchures," Kerry said, fluttering her sooty eyelashes for effect.

"Yeah, they'll practice their pucker." Misa made kissy noises, and they all busted up. *Ha-ha.*

The final bell dinged over the loudspeaker, and Mrs. Law looked up with her usual expression of shock.

"Well, hello, everyone." She stood as we swung around in our seats to face the front.

"I am sorry about earlier," Lori whispered from behind. "I know I was late, but we pulled it together. You sounded great."

No, I didn't. But I shrugged and reached into my pack for a pen.

"Come on, Tay," Lori whispered. "Don't be mad. Not when I'm so happy."

My shoulders felt stiff with anger, but I forced myself to breathe deep and let it go. After all, this was the first time *ever* that Lori had done something like this. Misa and Kerry were happy for her, and I knew I should be, too. I turned enough so Lori could see me nod. I even smiled a little.

She smiled back and squeezed my arm—it was the sign. We were cool again, back to normal.

Only, I didn't feel like normal.

The air conditioner would come on in the afternoon once the temperature heated up. But it wasn't on now, so the air was still and quiet. It didn't matter. Sometimes you couldn't feel the Winds of Change until it was too late.

♪ 9 ♫

It was nearly half an hour before school started on Wednesday, and already the band wing thrummed with music. The percussionists had taken over; drum riffs echoed down the hall from the open doors. All the practice rooms were booked solid, and muted sounds seeped into the hall from the mostly soundproofed rooms.

I just had to grab my ligature, and then I'd go meet Lori. I was pretty sure I'd left it in the practice room last night. I hurried to the third room and stood on my tiptoes to look through the small window in the door as I raised a hand to knock. I froze, my fist an inch from the door, and sucked in a breath.

Michael Malone. *Figures.*

He sat in front of a music stand so I could see him only from the side. I heard him stop, then start again. Then stop again. *Was Michael Malone face-scrunching?*

Suddenly, as if I'd thought it out loud, he looked up. Our eyes met.

Freakingtastic!

My cheeks fired with embarrassment—he probably thought I was spying. As if I would. *Well, maybe I would.* But I wasn't. I shoved open the door so hard it made a sucking noise as the air rushed out. "Sorry," I said, sticking my head in. "I left something in here last—"

He held up a ligature.

"That's mine!" I said, relieved. I stepped inside, the door swinging shut behind me.

"Yeah, I recognized the shine." He dropped it in my hand, the silver reflecting the overhead lights. "What do you do, use polish?"

"I just like to keep it clean. Which you might consider trying one day."

He set the clarinet on his knee and flashed me his I'm-too-cool smirk. "Still worried about my digestive enzymes?"

I slanted my eyes in a disgusted glare. "If you don't mind sounding spitty, then why should I care?"

His smile faded. He surprised me by looking right in my eyes. "You think I sound spitty?"

"*Yeah!*" I wanted to say. But it was a lie and I couldn't do it. "No," I muttered. "You don't."

"You don't sound spitty, either," he said. "Not that there's any spit inside your clarinet." But this time he said it with a real smile.

"Yeah, well." I shrugged. "I'm anti-spit. Just in general."

He nodded. "Me, I like a good spitting contest now and then."

"I can see that about you."

Our eyes met, and for a change, it didn't feel like a clash of competitors.

"Speaking of spit," Michael added, "what's the deal with Frank?"

I slid the ligature on and off my finger like a ring. Frank sat behind us and had a small saliva problem. "I don't think he closes his mouth all the way when he plays."

Michael blinked. "For real? Because I feel like I'm sitting in front of a sprinkler. I got to say something."

"You can't," I told him. "I don't think he can help it. He's got special rubber-band attachments on his braces."

"He's going to figure out something's wrong when I show up to band in a raincoat."

I laughed—it just sort of burst out of me, completely unexpected. Kind of like his sense of humor.

He grinned, and I suddenly understood what Lori might see in him. He had a nice smile—when he wasn't smirking.

I stuck the ligature in the pocket of my backpack. "I said the exact same thing about the raincoat to Aaron six months ago."

"Not surprised," Michael said. "You guys are pretty funny together."

"Who?" I frowned. "Aaron and me?"

"Yeah. You guys are always going off on something during band."

"I guess," I said. "We've known each other a while. Anyway, I think Frank's rubber bands come off in a month."

"I suppose I won't drown in a month." He shrugged and brought his clarinet back into playing position.

I pointed to the music stand. "Well. I'll let you get back to it." Then my jaw dropped as I got a good look at his sheet music. The page was full of black—which meant lots of fast passages.

"Is that your solo?" I asked. "It looks hard."

His eyes flickered back to the music. "More points, right?" But I saw a line between his eyebrows. Definite face-scrunching. All of a sudden, I remembered that first day in band and how he'd seemed nervous about the audition.

I licked my dry lips. "Lori told me your dad is a musician."

"Yeah," Michael said. "In New York."

"And you're going to play in his band?"

"That's the plan when I'm old enough."

I worked my hands into my back pockets. "That must be tough, though. Having him so far away."

"Yeah, it kind of sucks."

"Does he visit very much?"

"He can't," Michael said. "They've got gigs. But he'll come out if I make District Honor Band."

Frowning, I thought through what he'd just said. There was something weird about it. . . . "So," I asked slowly, "does that mean if you don't make it, he won't come out to see you?"

His fingers flashed white at the tips as if he were pressing them into the keys. "I didn't say that. I'm getting in, and he's coming out. End of story." Then he wet his reed and turned back to his music.

I swallowed, feeling like I should say something. But what? Instead, I backed out and closed the door softly until it clicked shut. I heard the muted sound of his clarinet again and stood there a minute, breathing hard. My heart felt heavy and fast, all at the same time. I wished I'd just gone in, grabbed my ligature, and walked out. I didn't want to know all that about his dad.

I liked Michael better when I could just hate him.

♪ 10 ♫

"You know a frog has three eyelids?"

I heard Aaron, but kind of like you hear a fly buzzing around your head. Like background noise.

"Uh-huh," I murmured, shifting on one of the high-backed chairs in the science lab. Luckily, Mr. Howard had assigned Aaron as my partner. Not only was he the smartest person in honors science, but he could make me laugh about anything—including frog guts. We'd been prepping our lab stations since Monday. Finally, we got to start dissecting today. I'd been waiting all year for this, and now I could hardly concentrate.

"Frogs lay thousands of eggs at one time," Aaron said.

"Huh." I took the study guide he held out, but the words were a blur on the page. Instead I saw flashes of thirty-second notes that I *still* couldn't play. On the back of my neck, I could almost feel Michael's hot breath as if he were getting closer and closer to beating me.

This morning had been weird. He'd been practicing an extra-hard solo so he could take *my* spot, and somehow I'd ended up feeling bad for him. Why did he have to go on about that dad stuff? Just because I asked didn't mean he had to tell me.

Besides, I had my own problems at home. And no way Michael was feeling sorry for me because my parents were separated. He didn't care that my mom had gotten a part in a community theater play, and in a few weeks, she'd be embarrassing herself on a stage as "Nurse Welty, Licensed to Kill." And what about Lori? Obviously he didn't care that I couldn't even talk to my best friend anymore. Her heart might be on my side, but her lips were on his.

"Did you know that when you slice open a frog, it farts?"

"Yeah," I said. Then I blinked. It took me a second to hear what Aaron had just said. "What?"

"Oh, so you're actually listening."

I rolled my eyes. "Jeez, Aaron."

"Just want to be sure you're awake before I hand you the scissors."

"Smart. Piss me off, then hand me a lethal weapon."

"Angry and out for blood," he said. "That's what I look for in a dissecting partner."

Before I knew it, I was smiling. "Idiot." I looked around for the first time. "So are we ready?"

The lab lights cast a white gleam on everything, making me wish I had sunglasses. Across from us, John and Spencer poked their frog with pins, even though we weren't supposed to touch them yet. I stared at ours, wrinkling my nose at the smell—sort of like Lysol but more intense.

Mr. Howard was still checking everyone's workspace. Ours had passed inspection. Frog on dissection tray. Aprons on us. Plastic gloves ready. Dissecting pins and scissors on the metal tray.

Finally, Mr. Howard cleared his throat. His polo shirt buttoned so high the collar bobbed up and down with his Adam's apple. "All right, everyone. We're ready to begin. Please refer to your worksheet and answer question number one."

Aaron held up the paper. "I don't believe this."

"What?" I leaned against his shoulder and read, "What sex is your frog?"

He frowned. "Isn't that a little personal? We've only just met."

I grinned and groaned at the same time. "We're not seriously supposed to look between its legs? How humiliating."

"For who?" Aaron asked. "Us or the frog?"

I looked at our frog—really looked. It had little legs with blue veins and a round white belly. I felt a

pang of sadness for it. I wouldn't like being mur-
dered so eighth graders could slice me open. The frog
might have had a nice lily-pad home and a best friend
before it was snatched. "We should name it," I told
Aaron.

"Why?"

"It seems nicer that way."

"It's nicer slicing open something with a name?"

"I don't know," I said. "It'll seem less dead that way."

"It's supposed to be dead."

"I know. It just looks so . . . previously alive."

"At least it died for science," Aaron offered, "a noble
and worthy cause."

"Yeah, and now we're sticking it with pins and checking out its privates."

Aaron laughed. "Well, we can't name it until we know
if it's a boy or a girl." He studied the worksheet. "We're
supposed to look at its fingers. Male frogs have thick
pads on the thumb."

"That's how you tell? The thumb?"

"That's what the paper says."

We both bent over the frog. "Are those thick?"

Aaron studied it a second longer. "I'm guessing it's a
male."

"Just to be safe, we'll call him Sam," I decided. "That
way it's okay even if we're wrong."

"So, Sam," Aaron said. "We're gathered here to slice
you open."

I shot him an evil look. "Is that your idea of kind and sensitive?"

"Just pretend it's someone you hate."

Immediately a pair of green-yellow eyes flashed in my head. "That's easy." I rolled one of the straight pins side to side on the tray.

"Let me guess," Aaron said. "Malone."

I nodded, thinking back to earlier. "I ended up talking to him this morning. I think he's worried about the audition, but he's still so sure of himself. It's incredibly annoying."

"Your frog is annoying?" Mr. Howard asked as he stopped at our table.

I looked up, startled. "Oh. Um. No," I stammered.

"Then what progress have you made?" he asked.

"Sam is a male," Aaron told him.

"Sam?" Mr. Howard repeated.

"We're on a first-name basis with our frog."

His mouth puckered around a smile. "I see. You may keep going." He walked to the next table, and Aaron leaned over the worksheet to write in our answer.

"He's not very good," he said.

I frowned at the stretched-out body. "We got a bad frog?"

"Not Sam," Aaron said. "Malone. He bangs out every note the same." Then he pushed back his hair so I could look right into his eyes, and he smiled. A very snarky smile.

A rush of True Like flooded through me—I really ought to create a whole new Level of Like in honor of Aaron. If we weren't sitting over a dead amphibian, I would have reached out and hugged him.

"If you've finished question one, please go on to question two," Mr. Howard called.

Aaron tapped the worksheet. "We're supposed to cut open Sam's mouth. You want to?"

My frog empathy evaporated in a little hum of excitement. I kind of liked cutting things open. Maybe it was having a big brother, but Andrew and I had cut open Barbie dolls and Beanie Babies and nearly every toy that came in a Happy Meal when I was little. I knew Aaron really wanted to do it, but I also knew he'd let me. "How about I start?"

We both pulled on our latex gloves. They clung to my palms like Saran Wrap and made sticky noises when I flexed my fingers. I grabbed the scissors and carefully sliced through the hinge of Sam's mouth.

"What's it like?" Aaron asked.

"Like cutting a piece of chicken."

We grinned at each other. I handed him the scissors. "Here, you do the other side."

He leaned over Sam, positioning the scissors.

"You know they're dating," I said.

"Lori and Michael? Yeah."

I flicked a fuzz ball off the table. "He didn't waste much time."

"Guess not."

"He also got the practice-room schedule changed so he could have more rehearsals."

Aaron's eyebrows shot up behind the screen of his hair. "Mr. Wayne did that for him?"

"He did it for Lori," I admitted. "She's the one who asked." I drew scratchy zigzags in the tray's paper liner with the straight pin. "I saw his solo music this morning. He picked something really hard, and now he wants Lori to help him. Instead of practicing with me yesterday, she helped him with rhythms."

"That's not cool."

I wiggled the pin through a tiny hole in the liner. "She couldn't say no. He's her boyfriend."

Aaron looked up, the scissors still in his grip. "That's total crap." Then he took aim and cut through the rest of Sam's mouth. Instead of flopping open, the jaw stayed in place. But the smell suddenly got a whole lot worse.

"That's disgusting," I said. "Talk about not moving a muscle."

"Rigor mortis," Aaron said as he made a note on the worksheet.

I ripped a slash in the paper. "Mr. Wayne said I should do a solo." It was the first time I'd said the words out loud. I still hadn't told Lori . . . or Mom and Dad. But it felt okay telling Aaron—he always acted like I could handle a solo with one hand tied behind my back. Still, my heart sped up just putting the words out there. "He picked one out for me," I added, glancing at my back-pack where I'd stuffed the sheet music in my English notebook. Mr. Wayne had handed it to me after band yesterday—*just in case*, he'd said. I hadn't even looked at it. But the harder I tried to forget, the more I couldn't stop thinking about it.

"You going to do it?" Aaron asked.

"It's too late to learn a solo."

"Wimp."

I elbowed him in the arm. "I'm not a wimp. I just need Lori to get focused."

"Like that's going to happen."

Before I could draw breath to argue, Mr. Howard raised his hand from the front of the room. "After you finish step two, you may begin to clean up. That's all we have time for today."

"We'll get it together," I said in a low hiss. "We always do."

"She blew you off yesterday to practice with Michael."

"She'll make it up."

"And she skipped your first play-through for Mr. Wayne."

"She didn't skip it; she was late. And I'm going to stop telling you things if you're just going to throw them back at me."

He opened the frog's mouth with his gloved fingers. "I'm just saying. It sounds like she's flaking out."

"She's not flaking out." I reached for a handful of pins. "At least, she doesn't mean to be."

While he held the jaw in place, I pushed in the straight pins to tack down Sam's mouth. "It's just different now that she has a boyfriend. He's always around. Even when he's not supposed to be."

"Like when?" Aaron asked.

"Like this Friday night."

"What's Friday night?"

"Basketball game. Lori and I signed up weeks ago to work concessions at halftime. Now he's going to want to work it with us."

Aaron made another note on the worksheet. "So hang with me instead."

I blinked, surprised. "Huh?"

He turned on his stool until he faced me, his navy board shorts skimming my knee. "At the basketball game. We can walk over together."

"But . . ." I took a breath. "I always go with Lori."

He tilted his head, studying me, his expression unreadable. "Maybe if you're not waiting around for her, she'll notice you're missing."

"No," I said, shaking my head. "I don't need to do anything like that." I peeled off a glove. "Lori already feels bad. She made a big deal at lunch today that I had to come over after school. I know she wants to make it up to me. So"—I shrugged—"thanks and all. But I'll see you there."

He twisted back toward the desk. "Sure. Whatever." Then he reached for the tray. "I'll take this up." A second later, he brushed by me, his eyes on the tray as he carried it to the front of the room.

I watched his stiff back and felt like I'd said something wrong. I just wasn't sure what.

♪ 11 ♫

I loved Lori's room.

With orange walls, a pink comforter on her white poster bed, and yellow pillows, it felt like I'd landed in a tub of rainbow sherbet. Best of all, there were two big cushy green chair pillows—the kind you could lean back on—set up in the corner.

Lori wasn't a star geek like me, but she'd let me stick a glow-in-the-dark galaxy on her ceiling anyway. Next to her bed, she had a calendar with pictures of the two of us on every month. I'd made it for her birthday. April's picture showed us in midair jumping off the Van Sants' diving board. We were holding hands and laughing.

I dropped into a chair and sighed. "Today took forever." I popped open a can of Diet Cherry Coke. Between the two chairs, Lori had set down a plastic bowl of microwave popcorn—the low-fat, air-popped kind. I missed the old days when we'd have had a bowl of grapes and a pack of Ding Dongs each. We'd finish the Ding Dongs, wad up the foil wrappers, and play marbles with them. The last time we did that was just after Thanksgiving. It made me sad now that I thought about it. No one warns you when you're doing something for the last time.

I munched a handful of tasteless popcorn while Lori grabbed a bowl of beads and the necklace she'd been working on. She'd made me an anklet last week as nice as the ones you buy at the mall. "Did you know that if you don't get enough salt in your diet, you can develop a goiter?" I said.

She blinked at me. "A goiter?"

"You know, a bulge on your neck. We learned it in science."

"That's disgusting."

"True. It's one of the things I love most about science. The disgusting factor." I wiggled my fingers around another handful of popcorn. "Speaking of necks, you should see Andrew's beard."

"Still growing?"

"I'd say like a weed except weeds are natural, and this thing definitely isn't."

She laughed as she worked a blue bead onto the wire. "Is the baseball team still winning?"

"Yeah, but today's game will be the big test."

She paused and rolled a yellow bead between her fingers. "Did you want to go?"

"You kidding?" I said. "I'd rather hang out with you."

She set the beads back in the bowl. "I'm so glad you came over. I still feel bad about not practicing with you yesterday."

I almost shrugged off the apology, but I stopped myself. Aaron was right—it hadn't been cool. "Yeah, me, too."

"Michael really needed the help."

I fiddled with a kernel of popcorn. "Funny how he needed it right when we were supposed to be practicing."

"Arc wc back to that again?" I heard the edge of annoyance in her voice, but I was annoyed, too.

"I just think it's suspicious. Why does he always seem to call when we're practicing, unless he's trying to sabotage me?"

"Sabotage?" She rolled her eyes.

"I'm serious. If he screws up our practices, then I won't be as sharp at auditions, and he has a better chance of making it."

Her jaw dropped. "You think he's just going out with me to mess you up?"

Hearing it back like that ... I winced. Maybe it hadn't come out right. "I didn't mean it that way."

"Then exactly how did you mean it?"

"I know he likes you," I said carefully. "I'm just saying the timing was suspicious."

"It wasn't suspicious," she shot back. "Michael tried to get a room later in the day, but Mr. Wayne didn't have any other openings."

"Okay, sorry, I didn't know." I tapped her foot with mine. "Forget I said anything."

She looked away a second, her fingers gripping the armrests. Then she sighed and turned back. "I'm sorry, too. But this means a lot to Michael."

"I know—it means a lot to me."

"But it's not just District Honor Band." Lori pulled her hair into a pony and twirled it around a hand. I could sense her sudden nervousness, feel it thrum through me as if we were connected. "Michael really wants to impress Dr. Hallady."

"So do I."

"But you don't," Lori said. "You hate Dr. Hallady."

"I don't hate him." I curved my arms around the fuzzy sides of the chair. "I hate that he's scary, and he makes kids cry during practices."

"Which is why it's good that you'll be in concert band with Mr. Gibbs—he's supposed to be really cool."

The thrumming inside me grew with my own nervousness. "Maybe I don't want to be in concert band. Mr. Wayne thinks I have a chance to make Wind Ensemble."

Surprise flashed in her eyes. "He said that?"

"If I do a solo and nail it, yeah."

"But you're not doing a solo." She stared at me as if she'd never seen me before. "What's going on with you, anyway? You never said anything about Wind Ensemble before this."

"Because I never thought I could make it. But I've been getting better—even you said so. And Mr. Wayne noticed, too."

Since the day I talked with Mr. Wayne, I hadn't been able to stop thinking about Wind Ensemble. It was as if he had lit this tiny flame inside the pit of my stomach . . . the beginning of a fire that hadn't quite caught hold yet. I'd been wrapping my arms around it all week, fighting my own worry to keep it alive.

Mr. Wayne believes. The flame glowed brighter, warmer, with the thought. But it wasn't enough on its own. I needed Lori to believe it, too, because if she did, then it would be real. I licked my lips, thinking that now I could tell her, make her understand. Now—

Beethoven's Fifth Symphony blared from the pocket of Lori's backpack. "Sorry," she said, crawling past me and reaching for her cell phone. "Hang on."

She looked at the screen and smiled. "Michael," she said, as she started typing. "He's getting his hair cut. I told him not too short."

She hit Send, then sat back down, reaching for her soda. "So what were we talking about?"

Me. Wind Ensemble. District Honor Band . . .

Before I could say a word, she waved a hand in the air. "Oh right. Michael and Wind Ensemble." She sighed. "I'm so glad I can talk to you about this and you understand."

I crumbled a kernel of popcorn in my fingers. "Understand what?"

She reached for my wrist and squeezed. "That you're my best friend, and that's not going to change no matter what."

"Oh-kay," I said, wondering why that made me more worried than relieved. "Is something going on?"

"Sort of, but nothing to freak out about."

I pulled my wrist free as my heart yo-yoed into my throat. "Why would I freak out?"

"Just promise me you won't."

I was now officially past freaked and hovering near panic. "Lori, what?"

"It's not going to change anything," she said, staring straight into my eyes. "Really. You and I are still on track with our duet." She took a breath. "But Michael asked me to do a duet with him for the audition, too. I couldn't say no."

♪ 12 ♫

He asked you to do WHAT?"

"Don't get mad!"

"Too late!" I snapped. Anger pulsed through me, and I shot to my feet. I paced in a circle—one hand pressed to my forehead—mostly so it wouldn't explode. "I told you he was trying to sabotage me."

"It's not like that. He's having a hard time with the solo. That's why he wanted me to help him yesterday. And it was a mess, Tay, embarrassing even. What could I do?"

I paused to fling my arms wide. "Tell him to keep practicing."

She gasped. "He's my boyfriend."

"And I'm your best friend."

"Do I have to choose?"

I paced another circle, then faced her again. "It's

District Honor Band, Lori. We're competing against each other." Angry tears pressed at the corner of my eyes. "You know he's my main competition and that if he gets in, I don't. And now you're going to help him get in?"

"It's not like that," she said. She punched a hand on the arm of her chair. "Would you please sit down so I can explain?"

I circled one more time, just to make the point, but then I gave in and sat down.

"I'm just his duet partner, Tay. He gets judged on his own playing."

"But you were my secret weapon."

"I still am."

"Not if you're playing for both of us."

Her shoulders suddenly drooped, and her eyes filled with tears. "This whole thing is so awful, Tay. I'm miserable."

I slid my hands to the carpet, trying to find something to hold on to. My head spun, and I felt like a balloon caught in a gust of wind . . . as if Lori had just let go of the string and I was spinning out of control.

"You're my best friend in the world," she said, blinking hard. "Of course I want you to make District Honor Band. I'd be completely lost without you."

I wanted her to reach for my wrist again. To pull me back down to safety. I grabbed a fluffy pillow that had fallen off her bed and hugged it close. "Then why did you say yes?" The anger was gone from my voice, leaving nothing but hurt.

"Because he needs me, Tay. It's not that I'm trying to harm *you*—it's that I'm trying to help *him*."

"But you can't do one without the other."

"Yeah, I can. If you think about it, I'm just the accompaniment. It's going to be about how well you play. How well you both play."

"It's not that simple."

"Why not?"

I slid forward. "For one thing, how will you have enough time to practice two duets along with your solo?"

"I'll make time. Your duet comes first—I told Michael that."

Did she? Her eyes were clear and steady, but I just didn't know.

"Michael and I are going to do the same duet you and I did last year," she went on. "I already know the flute part, so I won't have to practice it much."

"You've already got it all planned out?"

"Would you listen?" she said, frustration adding an edge to her voice. "The duet I'm doing with you is much harder. You'll get more points just on difficulty alone."

"If we practice enough for me to play it right."

"We will."

I shook my head, my heart in my throat. "You have to tell him no, Lori. You just have to."

"Why?" she snapped. "Because that would be better for you? What about me? He's my boyfriend, Tay. Did you forget that?"

"How could I?" I muttered. "You remind me ten times a day."

"And you said you weren't going to get weird."

"That was before I knew you were going to choose him over me."

"*Ugh,*" she groaned. She covered her face with her hands. When she shoved her fingers through her hair a second later and looked back up, her eyes had narrowed and her cheeks burned red. "I'm not choosing anything. You're the one who's making this into a choice. If I want to stay friends with you, then I can't have a boyfriend—is that what you're really saying? I never thought you'd be like this."

She stared at me, hurt, and the air whooshed out of me. "That's not what I meant."

"I always thought our friendship would last through everything, but now I'm not sure."

"Come on," I said, worry rushing in to fill my lungs.

"Do you even want to be friends anymore?"

"Of course I do!" Fear made my voice tremble. "You're getting this all wrong."

"Then you're not making me choose?" she asked.

My chest shook as though I were hyperventilating. Once, when I was five years old, I'd run into a swing post at a playground. When I stood up I was so dizzy,

Mom had me bend over and look at my fingers until I could count every one. I stared at my fingers now, but the dizziness was something different this time. Something inside me. "I can't believe this is happening."

"I know." Her face softened, and she reached for my wrist, squeezing in that way she always did; that way that said everything was okay. But suddenly I wondered if it really just meant everything was okay for Lori.

"I'm sorry," she said again. "I wouldn't do this if I thought it would hurt you. Honest," she added. "You're a better player. I've heard you both and you are."

I took in a long, shaky breath. I wanted to believe that—so much.

"I'm serious, Tay." She squeezed my wrist again. "You'll still make the band, but this way Michael won't be mad at me when you do. Is that so much to ask?"

Was it? I couldn't think straight, could only feel the reassuring pressure of her hand.

"I guess not," I said. If only I were as confident as Lori. My eyes throbbed with the pressure of unshed tears. "I count on you, Lori. You know that, right?" It came out all wobbly and lame and pathetic like I was four years old.

"I count on you, too," she said seriously. Like it wasn't lame and pathetic at all.

Then she reached over and hugged me. I hugged her back. I could feel the bones in her shoulders—hard

edges that hadn't been there before she'd lost the
weight. But it was still Lori. Still the one person I could
always reach out to.

"I knew you'd understand." She squeezed tighter.
"You're such a good friend that way."

Then Beethoven began playing again.

"Sorry," she said and pulled away. She reached for
her phone. I folded my arms around the pillow again.
"Michael," she said as she shot me a sorry look. Then
she turned back to the phone and started typing.

And without even thinking it through, I reached for
my own cell phone. I flipped it open and typed in Aaron's
number.

**Still want to go to the game together Fri?
I'm in if U R.**

♪ 13 ♫

The warm breeze swirled over my face like a blow-dryer as I pedaled up Dad's cul-de-sac Thursday after school. It felt good, though, to work my legs and suck down some non-air-conditioned air. The bushes had turned flowery and colorful in the past month, and I rode past a mix of yellow and pink, steering my wheels toward the few patches of shade from overhanging trees. Dad had left his garage door open, and I coasted up the bumpy pavers of his driveway and into the cool darkness.

Other than Dad's truck, the garage was empty and cleaner than the inside of most people's houses. Our garage at home was never clean. Tools, camping gear, and old truck parts spilled out of cabinets. It had gotten so bad, Andrew complained that taking out the garbage was like running an obstacle course. This didn't look like Dad's garage at all.

Maybe because he wasn't planning to stay?

The door to the house swung open and Dad stuck out his head. "Hey, Taters. Thought I heard you."

"Hi." I undid the chin strap of my helmet.

"I'm getting some things ready. Leave your stuff and come on in." Then the door thudded shut behind him.

I took off my helmet and set it on the handlebars. I shrugged the pack off my back, but I wasn't going to leave it in the garage—it held my clarinet and music. I reached for the door handle, but froze when I saw Dad's hiking boots.

For as long as I could remember, Dad's crusty old boots had sat outside the door to our kitchen. Mom would ask him to store them in a garage cabinet so she didn't have to smell them, but really they didn't smell, and Dad wouldn't do it anyway. He said he liked knowing they were ready whenever he was.

Hiking was one of his favorite things. He got out of whack when he flew overnighters, and lots of nights he couldn't sleep. So he'd put on a headlamp and go for a hike on the desert trails behind our house. Sometimes, when there wasn't school the next day, he'd wake me and I'd go with him. He'd carry the telescope, and we'd set it up at a curve in the trail and name the constellations.

I stared at the worn, brown leather and the dirt crusted onto the shoelaces and toes. We hadn't done a night hike since he'd moved out. These boots didn't belong here.

Neither did my dad.

I pulled open the door, and he stood there, smiling. Dad has a big smile that people say is his best feature, but I like his eyes best. When he laughs, they crinkle up like Chinese fans. But I wasn't in the mood to be smiling—or to see him smiling as if everything was fine.

"Come on in," he said.

I set my pack down carefully on the marble floors. I could see the laundry room off to my right, but I still couldn't picture Dad washing his own clothes. The kitchen was bigger than our kitchen at home, with glossy cabinets and fancy granite counters, but I still didn't like it. At home, Mom had hung yellow curtains, and blue rugs covered the wood floor.

The whole house was dark, shiny, and reeked of furniture polish. But Dad was not a polish kind of guy. He wore jeans when he didn't have to dress up for work, got dirty fixing cars, and kept filthy boots in the garage. The guy who lived here ought to sip wine and speak with an English accent.

How could he want to be that person? How could he want to live in this weird house while all of us were just two blocks away in a perfectly great *home*? It wasn't like Mom and Dad had fought all the time. It wasn't like she didn't want him back. Maybe she hadn't come out and said it, but why else was she so unhappy? Why else was she doing things like community theater with pathetic Mrs. Lansing?

"I thought we could bake a cake today," Dad said.

"A cake?" I made a face. "I should really practice."

"Come on, honey. It won't take long."

"How do you know?" I grumbled. "Since when did you ever bake a cake?"

"So it's time I learned." He gestured to the counter.

A pile of stuff sat next to the sink. I looked back at him. "Seriously?"

"I got a cake pan and mixing bowls." He picked an electric mixer out of the pile. "I even bought one of these."

He smiled, a hopeful look in his eyes. Then he reached into a cupboard and pulled out a box of angel food cake mix. "Your favorite," he added, wiggling the box.

I crossed my arms over my chest. "What's going on? This is not normal father behavior."

He leaned one hip against the counter. "Your mom thinks you're having a tough time. I thought if we had a chance to talk . . ."

"You mean you want to grill me for info?"

"That's one way of saying it." He set the box on the counter. "Mostly, I wanted to spend some time with you. Usually, we eat and you disappear with your clarinet."

"Maybe I don't want to talk."

"Then we don't have to. We could just make a cake." His green eyes smiled at me along with his crooked grin. Beard stubble shadowed his cheeks, and the Red Sox T-shirt I'd given him for his birthday hung in wrinkles over his jeans.

How could I say no with my dad looking at me like that? I sighed. "Okay, but I'm in charge because you'll mess it up."

He broke into a huge smile. For some reason, that made my throat tighten. He had so many lines crinkling up at the edge of his eyes—more lines than I'd seen in a long time.

"You be the captain," he said, "and I'll copilot."

I held out my hand for the cake mix. He passed it to me, and I read the directions. "You have eggs?"

He went for the ingredients while I ripped open the box.

"So auditions are a week from Saturday, right?" he asked.

I nodded.

"You ready?"

"Getting there."

He set the carton of eggs on the counter. "And you have a whole night at a hotel with all of your friends? You must be excited." He raised one eyebrow, like I should fill him in.

I ripped open the plastic wrap in the box and dumped the mix into a bowl. "Yeah."

"You know . . ." He straightened and drummed on the counter with his fingers. "I got you something. Maybe now is a good time to give it to you."

He disappeared into the laundry room. I waited, my hands around the glass bowl of cake mix, a few butter-flies of excitement flitting around my stomach in spite of my bad mood. *A present?*

A minute later, he was back, a small velvet box in his hands. *Jewelry?* I wiggled open the black lid. A gold charm bracelet lay inside, and attached was an engraved heart: HONOR BAND.

"Dad." I closed the lid, the butterflies dropping like dead gnats. "I haven't made it yet."

"I know," he said. "Mom told me I should wait, but you made it last year. Plus, I was afraid I'd be gone work-ing when you find out. This way, it can also be a good-luck charm."

"I hope you can return it," I said, handing it back to him.

"Why?" His voice deepened with surprise.

I studied the cake directions. "We need half a cup of water."

"Tatum!" He came up beside me and turned me with a hand on my shoulder. "What's going on? You've been talking about District Honor Band all year."

"Nothing's going on," I snapped. "I just may not make it."

"Does this have something to do with the new guy? Your mother told me there was a new clarinetist."

"Half a cup of water," I said again.

He didn't take the hint. Both of his hands circled my shoulders. "You're not just going to let him take the spot from you without a fight, are you?"

"It's not like we're going to wrestle for it."

"You know what I mean, honey. You have to believe in yourself. You have to go for it. Are you doing everything you can?"

"Yes." I pulled away, grabbing the measuring cup myself. As I filled it at the sink, a tiny traitorous voice piped up and asked, *Are you really doing everything you can?* The voice came from my backpack. From the solo music still stuck inside a folder. Mr. Wayne had said the music was singing my name. Maybe it was, because I swear, it kept calling to me. Maybe it was possessed. Maybe *I* was possessed. Only, if I were, I'd go demon on Michael and slice off his pouty lips.

I dumped the water into the bowl and stirred. "Can we just bake?"

"I'm trying to help, honey."

I dropped the whisk so that batter splattered on the cold, stone counter. "Well, you're not. If I make it, I make it. It won't be the end of the world if I don't." My words would've sounded impressive, too, if my voice hadn't cracked. "Your making a big deal about it just makes me feel worse."

He held up his hands. "Okay. I'm just worried about you."

"If you're worried, then why don't you move back home? Then I won't even care about stupid Honor Band."

He ran a hand through his hair. There was more salt than pepper in it now. "It's not that easy, Tatum."

"Is anything?" I mumbled.

I felt his hand on my shoulder again. "I love you, honey."

I handed him the measuring cup. "You can put this away."

"Yes, ma'am." He saluted me, then laid the cup on the drain board by the sink. He leaned an elbow on the counter and watched me stir. "That looks good," he said doubtfully.

"It's not done yet." I swirled the whisk around the bowl. "You know Mom got a part in that play?"

He nodded. "I know."

"She's a bodyguard pretending to be a nurse."

"It sounds interesting."

"It sounds lame." I stirred some more, though the batter had puffed up.

"Tatum," Dad warned. "You need to be supportive."

"She's going to dress up like a nurse, wave a gun, and say lines like, 'It's time for your shot.'" I rolled my eyes. "I cannot, in good conscience, support that." It was a phrase I'd heard Mrs. Law use before, and it had a nice ring to it.

Dad didn't look impressed. "Your mom is enjoying this—don't ruin it for her."

"She's only doing it because she's lonely." I gave him a pointed look. "If you'd just come home . . ."

He sighed, looking at me through sad eyes. "That won't solve things, Tay. Two people can be together and not really be together."

"What's that mean?"

"Well, we're trying to figure that out."

"But you're the parents. How can you not know?"

"That's a switch," he said. "I thought parents didn't know anything."

"But—"

He tapped on the box, not letting me finish. "What's next?"

I read the directions. "Three eggs."

"Aye, aye, captain." He flipped open the egg carton and pulled out three eggs.

"We have to separate them into a bowl."

He saluted me again, then got three cereal bowls out of the cupboard. "One egg in each bowl?"

I couldn't help it. I laughed. "That's not how you separate eggs."

"Are you making fun of me?" He pretended to put me in a headlock, but really he just rubbed my hair. His T-shirt felt warm against my cheek and smelled like his soap. "You love me, too?" he asked.

I reached around and hugged him. "A little."

He laughed into my hair, and we stayed like that for a minute. "The cake, Dad?"

He laughed again and loosened his hold. "So, what do you do with the eggs?"

I wiped a hand at the side of my eye and focused on the cake ingredients. "You have to separate the whites from the yolks."

"Oh," he said. "How do you do that?"

"Watch the captain." I cracked one egg, holding each side of the shell like a cup. I slid the yolk from one shell to the other, letting the white part fall into the bowl.

"Very cool," he said. "How did you learn that?"

"Mom taught me," I said. As I thought back, the memory filled me like an ache. My first angel food cake. Mom had let me carry it to the table, and Dad had pretended to choke from the first bite and fall to the floor. We'd all laughed, the four of us.

I felt a chill where I'd been warm a minute ago. Dad must have felt it, too, because he stiffened. "It was the first time I baked a cake for your birthday."

"Right." He slid his hands in his back pockets.

I grabbed the bowl with the yolk and dumped it in with the whites.

"Hey," Dad asked. "Why'd you do that?"

"I like them better when they're not separated."

⊚∕⊚

The closet seemed warmer than the rest of the house. It was more of a room than a closet—big enough for all of Dad's camping gear to fit in one end. Even so, it was kind of creepy, off by itself, upstairs in the back of the house. But I liked it. It was the one place in my dad's house I liked. You could shut the door and be in your own world. I brought my clarinet up here and practiced all I wanted and no one heard me but the shadows on the wall. In here, I was a famous clarinetist, renowned for my talent and beautiful hair.

There was only one overhead light, and I'd arranged an old camp chair beneath it. I propped open my folder of music on a cooler and pulled out the duet. The thirty-second notes stared up at me—black angry slashes on the page.

I was really starting to hate this duet.

A famous clarinetist wouldn't hate it. Then again, a famous clarinetist wouldn't be playing a duet. She'd be playing a solo. Without even meaning to, I reached for my English folder and thumbed to the back. There it was.

Clarinet Concerto by Mozart. Mr. Wayne had given me the second movement. I wondered what it would sound like and why he thought it was perfect for me. My mouth felt so dry, I ran my tongue over my lips, wishing I'd brought up a bottle of water.

I laid the music flat and looked at it. It wouldn't hurt to just try. The closet felt cozy with the door closed—like a cocoon. That made me smile. I was the caterpillar in my cocoon, and I could play inside as beautifully as a butterfly.

I filled my lungs with air and started slowly. The melody flowed out, raising goose bumps along my arms. The piece was a little sad, but a lot beautiful. I lifted my shoulders, imagining myself on a stage with bright lights above and a whole audience of Dr. Halladys listening. *Da dee de dee la la lee laaaaa.* The music built around me, and in my mind I could hear the audience murmur at my amazing talent.

I finished, listening as the last note echoed into perfect silence. Then the applause began. *Thank you. Thank you.* I bowed as the audience stood up, clapping and whistling.

If only.

If only I could play like I wanted to in my dreams, District Honor Band would be just the beginning. I'd try out for Wind Ensemble, and no one would imagine me not making it. Not even myself.

I folded up the solo and stuffed it away.

It was nice to dream about, but I couldn't stay in the closet where I was talented and brilliant and never got nervous. I had to face reality.

Lori and I hadn't talked again about her duet with Michael. But I'd thought about it all day. What happened if she started to like him even more? Would she give him extra help? Secretly want him to make it instead of me? I tried to stop myself, but the thoughts would push up like weeds, and when I yanked one out, another would shoot up. But I trusted Lori.

My stomach clenched. I had to.

I sank back into the shadows and went to work on the duet.

♪ 14 ♫

So when we get there," I said, "we'll pretend we're having a really great time." I dodged a pile of broken glass on the sidewalk and glanced over at Aaron.

He shot me a funny look. Well, maybe it wasn't a funny look. Maybe it was just that Aaron *looked* funny. Not *funny*, actually. Different.

"What?" he asked.

"Nothing," I said, realizing I'd been staring. It was almost seven, and the sun had just gone down. There were still a few streaks of red and orange painted across the clouds. Arizona had beautiful sunsets, but it was the pollution that caught the light and made all the colors. It was weird how something so good came from something so bad.

The streetlights had just clicked on, but it wasn't dark-dark. Not so dark that I couldn't see Aaron looked so not like . . . Aaron.

His hair, usually flopped over his eyes, had been brushed back over his forehead, the red highlights almost copper in the fading light. He'd even dressed different tonight, matching a gray polo and black jeans. He seemed taller and, I don't know . . . cool. Like if you didn't know who he was and you just saw him walking along the street, you'd peg him for a popular kid.

"You're staring again."

"Sorry," I said. "I just don't think I've ever seen you match before."

"That's because I'm color blind."

"Oh, Aaron." Embarrassment shot through me. "Really?"

"No." He smiled.

I shoved his shoulder, knocking him off balance for a second, and then we both laughed.

"I guess I never really cared about it before." He shot me a hesitant look. "But maybe I'll match more often."

I'd tried to look different, too. I wore a pink cami with a short white sweater that was more for fashion than warmth. I had on white capris, and I'd painted my toenails pink to match the cami. I wore my hair in a pony like usual, but I'd put clips in the front the way Lori said it looked best. I could feel the weight of it along the back of my neck, but in a good way. I still screwed up with eye pencil half the time, but tonight I'd done it right. I'd even managed to get the mascara on without stabbing my eyeball.

It was over a mile to the school, but I didn't mind the walk. Mom would pick me up after the game, or I'd call if I was going home with the Van Sants. It was kind of nice to walk. It felt normal—kicking rocks and looking up for the first sign of stars.

"By the way," I said, "thanks."

"For what?" Aaron asked.

His clarinet case bounced against his leg. Aaron played with the B-Rockers. They called themselves that because they played at school basketball games. There were only eight kids in the group, and they pulled on matching shirts and sunglasses every home game and played rock and roll during halftime. Mr. Wayne grumbled that the music would rot your ears, but he got the school to pay for the sheet music. They weren't bad.

"Thanks for thinking of this," I said. "You were right. I don't think Lori even realizes how she's been acting. If I say something, she thinks it's because I don't like Michael."

"She'll figure it out," he said.

"She better. I want things to get back to how they were." My voice caught as I thought of Mom. She'd been so happy today; I thought something good had happened with Dad. But it wasn't that at all. She'd gotten her nurse costume for the play.

"You okay?" Aaron asked. His eyes had dark rims around lighter brown irises—I'd never noticed before with his hair so shaggy.

"Yeah," I said. "I'm fine."

But those eyes wouldn't let go. He watched me as if he really saw me. As if he knew. It felt . . . I don't know. Not embarrassing like it should, but nice. Without meaning to, I said, "Actually, no. I'm not okay."

He nodded, but I could tell he was waiting for more.

"It's my parents. This separation is completely messed up. My mom is doing community theater, and my dad has this new job so he's hardly ever around. They say they want to work things out, but they never even talk."

I stopped and took a breath. Okay, now I felt embarrassed. What could Aaron do about it? What could he say that everyone else hadn't said a million times?

"Never mind," I said. "Forget all that."

Somewhere in the yard beside us, cicadas buzzed in chorus.

"Humans should be like wolves," he said.

I glanced at him, surprised.

"Gray wolves mate for life. Did you know that?"

I nodded, suddenly understanding. "Yeah. I saw the same show on Discovery."

"I thought about that show a lot when my parents split."

His voice was low and quiet, but his words worked through me, reaching someplace deep inside. "How long ago?"

"Three years." He kicked at a rock, and it danced

across the gutter. "Wolves don't divorce and send the cubs back and forth every other weekend and twice a month on Wednesdays."

"If wolves can do it, why can't our parents?"

"Exactly. Wolves probably have brains the size of a tennis ball."

"Maybe we should have been born wolves."

Aaron sighed. "Occasionally, they like to eat their babies."

"That's a downside."

We laughed, and the knots in my stomach loosened a little. The sound felt good—like music.

We crossed a street, the sky a plain, dark gray now, the sun shining on some other part of the world. "I keep thinking they'll work things out."

"I used to think that, too," he said.

"But it could still happen with my mom and dad. It's only been a couple of months."

He didn't say anything. I thought maybe he nodded, or maybe I just wanted him to nod.

"Did your parents try to work it out?" I asked.

"Not really. It was kind of too late by then. My dad remarried a year later, and that was that. My mom dates—it's like auditions for a new dad every year."

"How can you joke about it?"

"I don't know. I just do."

"I couldn't," I said. "If they split, I won't be able to handle it."

"You just think that," he said. "But your parents aren't together now, and you're doing okay."

"I don't feel okay."

He gave me a half smile. "That doesn't mean you're not handling it."

The way he said it, I wondered if maybe he was right.

"Besides," he added, "it could be worse. If our parents were wolves, they'd chew up our food for us."

I rolled my eyes, but I smiled, the way I knew he wanted me to. The thought popped in my head—that Aaron was always doing that, making me laugh when I needed it. "You're a good guy, Aaron."

His cheeks reddened. "Just don't tell anyone."

I was still smiling as we turned a curve in the road. Then I saw the school lights just above the rooftops and realized we were only a block away. My body tensed again—how had that mile gone by so fast? We crossed the last street and muffled noises grew louder—shouts and hollers and car doors slamming as parents dropped off kids. Music blared from the gym, and I could see the yellow bus that had brought the Ironwood Sparrows— our competition. Somewhere inside, Lori waited, hopefully missing me. Time to see if the plan had worked.

Never once did I stop to wonder if Lori might have been making plans, too.

♪ 15 ♫

Aaron and I crossed the parking lot, my gaze fixed on the gym doors. "Eyes on the prize," as Dad would say. Dad was all into visualization. You pictured good things happening in your mind, and then they happened. He said it worked so well that athletes hired visualization coaches. Now, before every game, Andrew visualized himself throwing strikes—at least, he had before the Beard.

The single, straggly chin hair had grown during the past week, along with the belief that it was somehow responsible for the team's winning streak—now in week two, with four wins. When Andrew's buddies came over, the first thing they'd do is squint at his chin, nod encouragingly, and say, "Dude!" I had a seriously hard time not puking whenever it happened. The hair had darkened and jutted out of his otherwise completely smooth skin—as if an eyebrow had lost its way. Emily had threatened to yank it, and they'd had a fight about it on our front lawn. Emily didn't want to take the backseat to a hair, and Andrew wasn't changing anything (except *maybe* his underwear), after going seven innings and giving up only two hits in Adobe's big game on Wednesday.

Unless the chin hair could vaporize a certain clarinet player from Dallas, I wasn't too impressed. I was sticking to visualization. If it worked for athletes, why couldn't it work for best friends? So I made my way through the rows of cars and visualized Lori waiting for me at the gym doors. I even visualized exactly what she'd say when she saw me.

"What took you so long? I've been waiting. I sent you a text—didn't you get it?"

I'd shrug. *"Oh yeah. Forgot to text back. You've been forgetting things lately, too."*

Then she'd blush. And she'd realize what she's been doing. And she'd grab my arm and it would be Tay-Lo again, the way it had been every Friday night before Michael moved in.

Thanks to visualization, I knew exactly how it would go.

But when we got to the gym, Lori wasn't there. "You see her?" I asked Aaron.

"Maybe she's waiting inside," he said.

I pushed through the lobby doors, barely getting in

around the crowds. I strained to see, even jumping to look over heads, but none of the kids hanging out were Lori. Or Michael.

"Let's check concessions," I called over my shoulder. I wove my way to the far end of the lobby. The concessions table sat near the wall, stacked with the usual candy bars and mints, along with coolers of Gatorade and bottled water.

Kids pressed forward in a crooked line and Steph, our one-and-only oboe player, manned the table. Behind her, Lori and Michael stood together, talking. She laughed at something Michael said and flicked a cube of ice at him. My heart dropped. She hadn't even noticed I wasn't there.

"You okay?"

I looked over. I'd forgotten about Aaron, but he'd come up next to me, his clarinet tucked under one arm.

"No." Someone bumped me, and I turned to glare. But it was Brandon, and he'd already moved off.

Lori looked up just then and saw me. Her smile widened. "Hey, Tay, there you are. Hey, Aaron," she added. Then she shrieked and grabbed her back.

Michael grinned. "Paybacks."

Lori fished a piece of ice out of her shirt. "You're going to suffer for this!"

I blinked hard. So much for visualization. "What are you doing?" I asked, trying to keep my voice steady. "We're not on concessions until halftime, right?"

She smoothed out her shirt. "Yeah, but there's such a big crowd Mr. Wayne asked for more help."

"He always asks for more help. I thought we'd hang out."

She lifted her eyebrows. She'd worn her hair in a French braid again, only she'd left wispy curls by both ears. Blue eye shadow sparkled on her lids, matching her blue lacy top. A new one. For some reason, that stung deep—she was shopping without me now, too?

"You weren't even here," she said.

I swallowed. This was it. The part where she noticed I had a life of my own. "I walked over with Aaron."

She shot a look at Michael, and he grinned back at her. "Told you," he said.

Told her what?

Then Michael leaned forward and fisted his hand so his knuckles faced Aaron. "Nice."

Nice, WHAT? Aaron tapped knuckles with him, but then he looked at me and rolled his eyes. "I'm going to put my clarinet down."

"Yeah, great." I wanted him gone so I could forget the whole stupid plan. It hadn't gone right, and now Lori and Michael were working concessions and dropping ice down each other's backs and telling secrets.

"Okay," I said to Lori, trying to sound matter-of-fact. "So you'll get double hours for working pregame and halftime."

"Oh yeah," she said. "About that." She glanced at

Michael, then grabbed my wrist. "Back in a sec," she called over her shoulder.

Then she half dragged me down the hall, ignoring Misa who was yelling, "Tay-Lo!" Lori pulled me around the corner and down another long hall until we'd almost reached the locker area and the roar of noise had dimmed to a rumble.

I took a deep breath and braced myself. If only I knew what I was bracing myself *for*.

"So," she said, "since I'm working now, Michael and I thought we'd skip halftime." She waved her hand in front of my face. Something flashed blue and black.

"What's that?"

"A bracelet. From Michael." Her eyes practically danced out of her face. "He wants everyone to know I'm his girlfriend."

It was a plain black cord with two blue beads that wrapped around her wrist and then tied in a knot. It was cheap and ugly. "Nice," I said around the lump in my throat.

She ran a finger under the cord. "You know what Michael said earlier? It was something about you." She took a breath—for dramatic purposes, I was pretty sure.

"He said he thought something was going on with you and Aaron. I said no or you would've told me. And then you showed up with him tonight."

Now it made sense, the look they'd exchanged when I walked up with Aaron. I should tell her the truth—Aaron was just a friend. But I paused a second, because she looked so curious. Why shouldn't she have a turn feeling left out and clueless? So I paired a closed-mouth smile with a tiny shrug. "Maybe I haven't told you everything."

For a second, she looked shocked. And I thought, *There, we're even!*

Then she smiled.

Smiled?

"That's awesome!"

"It is?"

Her smile widened and she laughed. "Now we can double-date."

I choked on a breath of air. "What?"

"You and Aaron, me and Michael. This is so perfect!"

I blinked, trying to think as fast as Lori was talking. But she'd already rushed on.

"Tomorrow night. The movies. My mom said I could only go if it was part of a group. So if you and Aaron come . . ." She squeezed my wrists. "We can hang out, the four of us. I've got to tell Michael he was right. This is so great!"

In two seconds, she'd disappeared back down the hall. My brain felt like a DVD that kept skipping back a scene. *Double-date?* I closed my eyes, pressing my hands to my temples, but it didn't stop the dizziness. I felt hot. Could I be sick? Could I be hallucinating all this?

Oh please, make this be a terrible dream. I sagged against the wall, wishing I could go home, bury myself under my comforter, and pretend none of this had happened.

But I couldn't. I straightened and took a shaky breath. I had to find Aaron and ask if he could go to the movies tomorrow night.

But first, I had to tell him we were dating.

♪ 16 ♫

Halftime was almost over. Through the open gym doors, I could hear kids chanting the fight song, gearing up for the second half. I'd sold concessions for a while, but there were lots of volunteers tonight, and no one cared when I snuck outside. I needed time to think. A decade would've been nice, but I was only going to have a minute or two. I had to go back inside and find Aaron.

I pulled the edges of my sweater together, glad now that I'd worn it. The night was cool—the gym nothing but a dark shadow behind me. I couldn't see the track field just over the hill, only a flicker of white from the tennis courts off to the right. A few stars were visible now, and a thin moon hung low like a crooked smile.

As if there was anything to smile about.

I wasn't sure where Lori and Michael had gone. Probably out here somewhere, kissing in a dark corner.

Maybe Lori could give Michael an intensely painful can-ker sore? Okay, so that was worth a smile.

I leaned back against the low brick wall that ran between Dakota Middle School and Tonalea Elemen-tary. I braced myself with my hands and looked up at the sky. The North Star was easy to spot without a telescope—Dad had showed me that. For centuries, people had counted on the North Star to show them the right way.

Me, I'd been happy to follow Lori.

I just never thought I would end up here.

I shouldn't have lied about dating Aaron. But then again . . . I remembered the excited look on Lori's face, the way she grabbed my wrist.

A cheer erupted from the gym, and the wave of sound reached all the way to my little wall. The second half must have started. I focused on the North Star again, pretending the bluish light was Aaron's face.

"So. Aaron," I said out loud, testing the words. "You up for a movie tomorrow?"

Even though I tried to sound normal, I didn't. At least, not to my own ears. The whole thing was too weird. I'd never asked a guy out for real. How was I going to ask a guy out for pretend?

My only romantic experience was with Brian Phelps in the sixth grade. We'd gone steady for three days and never actually talked. It was all done through text mes-sages. Including the breakup. Afterward, I didn't know how to act around Brian, so I avoided him.

I didn't want to have to avoid Aaron.

I fixed my eyes on the sky again, and in a much more normal voice, I said, "So. Aaron. I'm hoping you can help me out."

"With what?"

I shrieked and spun around. Aaron stood there, the red band shirt he'd pulled on for halftime shimmering in the weak light coming from the parking lot.

"You scared me." I laid a hand on my chest. My heart thudded as loud as a basketball hitting the gym floor.

"How could I scare you?" he asked. "You were talking to me."

"I didn't know you were there."

"Then why were you talking to me?"

"Because I—" I blew out a breath and ignored the way his eyebrows had slanted in a confused V. "What are you doing out here anyway?"

"Looking for you." He worked his hands into the pockets of his jeans. "To see how things went with Lori."

"Oh." I licked my lips. "Not exactly like I planned."

"What happened?" He sat down next to me on the wall.

"Well," I began, "we got into this discussion about boyfriends, and by the end of it, she kind of got the idea you and I are dating."

He blinked, his lashes a shade darker than his eyes. Confused eyes. "How'd she get that idea?"

I twisted my fingers together. "Because when she asked me if we were, I didn't exactly say we weren't."

"You told her we're dating?"

"No."

He paused a second with his mouth halfway open. "So you didn't say we're dating, and you didn't say we're not dating."

"Exactly."

"And from that, she decided we're dating?"

I half groaned, half laughed. "I guess Michael said something to her about us being more than friends. Then tonight, you and I walked in together. So she asked me about it, and I let her assume we were—just so she'd know I had secrets, too."

"She thinks I'm your secret boyfriend?"

"Yep," I said. "And she's very excited about it. She wants us to go on a double date tomorrow night. To the movies."

"Huh."

I wiped my palms on my capris. How could my hands be sweating when the rest of me was cold? And what did "huh" mean? I tried to read his expression, but he tilted his face up to the stars.

I followed his gaze and sighed. I loved how the pinpoints of light looked like freckles on the face of the sky. "Sorry about this," I said. "I keep trying to fix things, and they end up worse."

He stretched out his legs. "So why don't you just tell her the truth?"

"What truth?"

"That she's been ditching you and you're mad."

"Because I want her to figure it out on her own."

"I don't get that."

"That's because you're a guy."

"A guy would tell his buddy to stop being a jerk."

"Right," I said, rolling my eyes. "You always tell everyone exactly what you think."

It was too dark to see, but I was pretty sure his cheeks had just turned red. And he suddenly seemed all interested in the sky again.

"So what are you looking at, anyway?" he asked.

"The North Star." I pointed. "It's the end of the handle of the Little Dipper."

"That one?"

I nodded. "I could just tell her you can't go."

"But she'd still think we're together, right?"

I kicked at the base of the wall. "Would that be the worst thing? If people thought we were?"

"I don't know. Would it?" he asked, a funny catch in his voice.

He probably thought I was crazy to ask. Maybe I was. "I just want things to be the way they were. Nothing has felt right since Michael moved here."

As I said the words, I realized it was a lot more than that. It was Lori losing weight and changing into someone I didn't always recognize. It was Dad moving out, and Andrew sleeping over there, and Mom gone to rehearsals, and the house always empty. It was my whole family shifting away from me in every direction. And now Lori was moving further away, too . . . slipping out of my reach. It wasn't enough to try and hold on. I had to catch up—or I'd be left behind.

"If I have a boyfriend," I told Aaron, "then we're equal again. And nothing has to change."

He smoothed back his hair. "Obviously, you never went to science camp, or you'd know about the Uncertainty Principle."

"I don't like the sound of that," I muttered.

"It just means you can't predict how things will react, because everything changes. Even the stars change."

I shook my head. "Not to me they don't. Yeah, they may move across the sky, but they move together. It's not like the Big Dipper says, 'See ya,' and takes off without the Little Dipper."

He smiled. "You're really into astronomy, huh?"

"My dad got me started. He told me about the constellations when I was little, only he called them families. Star families. I always liked that."

The noise from the gym had died down, and I could hear Aaron sigh softly. He looked older with his hair pushed back, and it was kind of nice to see his face when I talked to him. It was a nice face—wide-set eyes, straight nose, and his lips were . . . well, nice. *What is it with me and Aaron's lips?* I looked away and twisted my fingers together.

"You know," he said, "we could go to the movies tomorrow night."

I gave him a hopeful look. "Really?"

"But we'd have to act different, right? As if we liked each other?" I could see the gleam of his eyes as he studied me. "Could you do that?"

"It would be easy since we're such good friends," I said. "Unless . . . do you think you could?"

"Yeah," he said softly. "I think so."

"It wouldn't have to be weird," I added. "We'll just be ourselves, except maybe we'll hold hands or something."

"Yeah?" he asked. "Like this?"

Before I could react, his fingers slid around mine. My breath caught as I felt a flash of warmth. Then a shock sparked from his hand to mine. I jerked my hand back. "Ouch! You gave me a shock."

"I think that means we have good chemistry."

"Or static cling." My heart hopscotched across my chest. I scooted down the wall, putting space between us.

"It's still chemistry."

"So I'll wear gloves tomorrow." I crossed my arms, balling my hands into fists, and tried to breathe normally. It was Aaron, I reminded myself. Just *Aaron*. We'd worked in science lab with our shoulders pressed together and whacked each other's knees in band a million times. If we had chemistry, I'd have known it. It was just a regular shock—I got those all the time.

But I don't usually still feel the tingles a whole minute later.

"Maybe it's better if we don't hold hands," I said.

"That bad?" he asked.

I looked into his eyes and suddenly wished he hadn't changed his hair or dressed nicer or showed up looking so . . . *good*. "I don't want to make things weird with us, okay? You're my friend, Aaron, and I'd be a wreck without you. I mean, who else could I ask out on a fake date?" I laughed a little, but deep down I was dead serious. I'd shared stuff with Aaron I hadn't even told Lori. "It'll only be for a few days," I promised. "On Sunday I'll tell Lori that we broke up."

He got quiet for a second, then said, "We're only going to last for two days?" But I heard the note of teasing in his voice. "How'd we break up?"

I managed a normal breath. "Does it matter?"

"I don't want your friends thinking I'm a bad boyfriend."

"I'll tell everyone you totally rocked. I'll blame it on my mom and say she got mad because I'm not allowed to go on dates until high school."

"Really? You're not?"

"No, I can." I frowned. "At least, I think I can. It's never come up."

"Why not?"

"Because there's no one I've wanted to go out with." I studied him a minute. "Why? Have you gone out before?"

"Yeah," he said. "I had a girlfriend."

"You did? Who?" I couldn't keep my voice from

rising. *Aaron had a girlfriend?* I couldn't picture it. Well, maybe I could—I'd just never tried to before.

"A girl at my temple."

"You went *out*, out?"

"We hung out at bar mitzvah dances, temple parties, stuff like that."

I squinted at him, not because it was dark, but because I felt like I was looking at someone I hadn't seen before. "So what happened?"

"I started liking someone else."

"Who?"

"Just . . . someone else." He stood up and glanced at the gym. "I'd better get back. I left my clarinet in the stands."

I stood up, too. "Okay. And thanks again for doing this. I owe you."

He started toward the gym, then stopped. I watched him slowly turn back to me, his face hidden in shadow.

"You know, Tay"—his voice was low, almost like it was part of the night—"if you spend all your time looking at the stars, you might miss what's going on right in front of your face."

Then he disappeared into the dark.

♪ 17 ♫

Mom?" I called. I ran down the stairs and around to the kitchen. Empty—just the slosh and hum of the dishwasher. We had to pick up Lori in fifteen minutes, or we'd be late for the movie. "Mom?" I called again.

I glanced at the hall clock as I jogged for her bedroom. I'd wasted forever looking for something decent to wear. I knew I had a crappy wardrobe, but tonight I'd hit a new low when I discovered a Hello Kitty T-shirt still hanging in the back of my closet. How was I supposed to fake-date without the right clothes? I'd finally settled on jeans and a green cami, figuring no one would notice because they'd be staring at my shiny, smooth hair. Except racing around the house in a panicked sweat was ruining the look (which took thirty minutes with a hair straightener!). No way was I going to be ready in time.

"MAHHHHHHM!" I scanned her empty room.

"In here," she called from the direction of the bathroom.

I rounded the corner, and had just a second to register Mom standing by one of the double sinks. Then she whipped around, lunged forward, and shoved a squirt gun in my face. "Hold it, Babyface," she hissed.

I gasped and tripped backward two steps.

This person—who I would never admit was my mother—stood decked out in a white dress, thick tan panty hose, and the ugliest white shoes I'd ever seen. She wiggled the gun and grinned. "What do you think?"

"You look like James Bond in a nurse's dress."

She straightened and posed with the gun by her face. "Bond," she said in a low voice. "*Jane* Bond."

I groaned. "Promise me you'll never do that voice again."

She laughed. "I'm just trying to get into character."

Mom didn't look like herself, that was for sure. Her brown hair usually hung straight to the top of her shoulders, but she'd pinned it back in a bun. Her cheeks were accented with blush, and she'd outlined her lips in deep plum so her teeth looked really white.

I watched as she picked up something that could have doubled as a basketball net, and fitted it over her hair.

"What is that thing?"

"It's a hairnet, part of my costume." She turned to

face me, her eyes glowing as bright as the mounted vanity lights. Or maybe it was all the purple eye shadow she'd put on. "I get to whip it off in the final act when it's revealed that I'm actually a bodyguard."

I groaned again. It was either that or scream.

"It's a very interesting story," she said. "A billionaire widow lives in a nursing home when she meets one of the residents and they fall in love. But her children are afraid he'll get her money." Mom tapped her chest with the barrel of the gun. "I pretend to be her nurse, but secretly I'm there to keep this man away. With force, if necessary." She grinned. "I'm just not sure where to carry the gun. What do you think? Should I strap it to my leg with a garter?"

"No!" I cried. "You cannot do that. You're my mother."

"So?"

"So mothers do not wear garters and strap-on weapons." I paused as a sudden horrified thought flashed through my brain. "You're not going out in public like that?"

"As a matter of fact," she said, turning back to the mirror, "yes, I am."

"Tonight?"

She leaned in closer and smoothed the blush at the top of her cheeks. "Mrs. Lansing and I are meeting a couple of the other cast members for coffee."

"In your costumes?"

"We're going to try and stay in character. It's a

dramatic exercise." She wiped a streak of plum lipstick off her tooth. "I'm looking forward to it."

"You *are*?"

She glanced at me, annoyed, then adjusted the hairnet so her ears popped out. "Aren't you supposed to be getting ready?"

I blew out a breath. "I can't find my eye pencil. Can I use yours?"

"It's in the top drawer," she said, gesturing. Then she tucked the gun in the thin white belt around her waist.

I rummaged through her makeup and found the smoky brown pencil. Out of the corner of my eye, I watched her dab lip gloss with the tip of her pinky.

"I didn't know you liked acting so much," I said. I ran the pencil along the inside of my bottom eyelid, then halfway along the top.

She put the cap on the lip gloss and leaned her hip against the counter. "It's something new, I admit. But why not give it a try?"

"Because you have to get up on stage looking like that. What if it's stupid?"

"Well," she said slowly, "then I guess I look stupid."

And even with all the bright purple makeup, her eyes seemed a little scared.

"Hold still," she said softly. She leaned forward, and I felt her finger at the corner of my eye, smoothing out the pencil. "I don't know how this will turn out," she admitted. "Maybe it won't be for me, but even if it isn't,

I'm still going to be glad I did it." She straightened the strap of my cami. "After all, how will I know what I can or can't do, if I don't go out and try?"

"I guess," I said. But I shuddered.

Mom laughed. "This from the girl who's going on a pretend date so she can hang out with her best friend who's dating a beady-eyed gorilla."

I looked at myself in the mirror and sighed.

Maybe acting ran in the family.

♪ 18 ♫

The night began perfectly. Lori met me at her door, nearly shaking with excitement. "Hurry," she'd said. "Before my dad changes his mind." We'd run down her sidewalk, arm in arm, laughing about nothing. An earlier rain shower had left everything clean, and the air smelled of possibility. If you wanted to get technical, the air actually smelled like the purple lantana in Lori's yard, but to me, tonight, it seemed like excitement flowed from us and into the atmosphere.

Even if you ignored the part where this was our first ever double date (*as if*), tonight was still a major deal. This was the first time our parents had let us go to the movies on a Saturday night by ourselves. Even my nerves over the fakery couldn't stop the adrenaline that ran through me as the theater rolled into sight.

Rock music blared from speakers, and swinging

lights flashed across the crowded parking lot like a Hollywood premiere. I sat up higher, crossing a leg underneath so I could get a better view out the window as the car dipped in a rut and then bounced up. Groups of kids stretched along the sidewalk from the bookstore down past the yogurt place, the taco shop, the coffeehouse, and even beyond the actual movie theater.

Lori turned to look at me, and she grabbed my wrist for a quick squeeze. I nodded, wishing I had a camera so I could have a picture of this exact moment.

"This is ridiculous," Mom said, craning her neck to see around the SUV ahead of us. Thankfully, she'd agreed to take off the hairnet for the drive over, and I didn't think Lori had noticed the nurse's dress. "The parking lot is wall to wall. Is every kid in Phoenix here?"

"Yep," we said in unison.

Mom's eyes caught mine in the rearview mirror. "I don't know if this is such a good idea."

"Mom!" I leaned forward until my seat belt stopped me. "You promised."

"I know, but . . ." Her gaze shifted to the crowds as we slowly rolled forward, the traffic moving by inches.

The sidewalks grew more and more crowded the closer we got to the theater. Up ahead, police cars were stationed along the curb, blue and red lights flashing for security.

"These kids all look like high schoolers," Mom said, shaking her head.

"Look." I pointed out the window. "There's Travis and Jerry and Caleb and Gavin. You know Gavin's mom, Mrs. Norton. They're all middle schoolers."

We passed the coffeehouse. Mom's hands tightened on the steering wheel. "Your mother is picking up after the movie, right, Lori?"

Lori nodded. "I'll call as soon as it's over."

"All right, then." Mom rolled to a stop at the edge of the theater. "This is as close as I can get. Have fun and make good decisions."

We were already halfway out of the car. "We will. 'Bye, Mom."

"Thanks, Mrs. Austin."

As soon as Mom drove off, Lori grabbed my arm. "Can you believe we're actually here? How does my hair look?"

"Disgustingly perfect." She'd curled the ends so they just reached the top of her shoulders—bare except for the lacy straps of a red cami she wore over her jeans. Well, over *my* jeans. They fit great, too.

"Let's find Michael," Lori said. "He texted that he's here."

He was waiting in front of the theater, slouched against a pillar in black cargo shorts and a skater tee. His shoelaces were untied. Of course.

"Hey," he said to me. Then he grinned at Lori. "You look hot."

Lori blushed and slid her hand into his. Part of me

wanted to roll my eyes, but another part of me felt sick at how Lori looked at him. As if she were a Disney princess and Michael was her prince. I should be happy for her—I wanted to be—but I just felt stupid and . . . forgotten.

I turned away and spotted Aaron. I waved, feeling better as soon as he saw me and smiled. He walked over, his hair brushed back again, looking good in a green polo. My heart thumped. Looking very good. I'd be so nervous if this were a real date, but it was just Aaron, I reminded myself. *Slow down, heart!*

"Hey," he said. He stopped next to me, his hands shoved deep in his pockets.

Michael grinned at us like he owned the world. Then he threw an arm over Lori's shoulder like he owned her, too. "So. You ready?" he asked.

Without missing a beat, Aaron swung an arm over my shoulder. "Born ready," he said.

It was the most insanely stupid thing I'd ever heard Aaron say. But a flutter rushed through me. It sounded cool. *He* sounded cool. And I liked how it felt—his arm over my shoulder. There wasn't a shock this time, only the spread of warmth from where his arm touched me. A melty warmth that made my breath catch. Lori wiggled her eyebrows as if she could tell.

Was I blushing? Because if I was, I had to stop. This was all part of an act.

As soon as Lori and Michael were a couple steps

ahead, I slipped out from under Aaron's arm. "Thanks," I whispered.

"You look nice," he said.

"You don't have to say that. They can't hear you."

"Okay." He ran a hand through his hair. "You look like a troll."

I laughed, relaxing again. "So do you. Guess it's a good thing we're together."

He smiled slowly. "Yeah. It is."

Just like that, another fluttery feeling wound its way to the pit of my stomach.

I led the way into the lobby.

♪ 19 ♫

Green," Michael guessed. He flashed open his eyes.

"Nope," Lori said with a grin, "pink."

"Dang," he muttered as he grabbed the bag of jelly beans. "Your turn."

We sat around a cement table in the courtyard in front of the theaters. If possible, it felt even more crowded than before the movie. Lori had called her mom, and it would be twenty minutes before she got here. So we'd filled bags from the candy store, and Michael had challenged Lori to a game of "guess which color jelly bean."

"Close your eyes," he said, "and open your mouth."

I wondered if Aaron thought this was stupid, but he smiled as he chewed his way through a gummy worm. He'd sat on my right during the movie, and Lori had sat on my left. Once, I felt an arm on my shoulder and nearly knocked over the popcorn when I jerked up. But it was Michael who had reached too far.

Now, he laid a jelly bean on Lori's tongue. She swirled it around, her lips twitching. "Blue."

"How does it taste blue?" he asked.

"Like ice," she said as she opened her eyes. "Am I right?"

"Lucky guess."

She laughed and raised her hand for a high five, which I was there to deliver.

A rumble of wheels grew louder, and I looked up as a guy skated by. Michael followed him with his gaze, watching as the guy crouched, then jumped a curb.

"Nice," he said. "You skate, Aaron?"

"Nope," Aaron said.

"Some people like to study the laws of physics," Michael said with his smirk. "Others like to defy them."

I rolled my eyes, but Aaron just leaned back, cool as could be, and popped a gummy worm in his mouth. "But you don't defy the laws of physics. You use them."

Michael laughed. "Yeah? What do you know about it?"

Aaron pointed toward the skater, who had just rolled out of sight. "I know he'll never get any height on an Ollie if he doesn't work on a lower center of mass."

Michael's eyebrows shot up. "I thought you didn't skate?"

"I don't. It's simple physics. Before the jump, he's at a zero net force. He needs to create lift."

"What about a 180?" Michael quizzed, leaning forward.

"Rotational inertia," Aaron said. "It's pretty elementary stuff." He shot me a quick smile, then rattled off some more big words. I flashed bug eyes at Lori and tried not to laugh out loud. Lori looked as amazed as I felt.

When Aaron finished, Michael reached a fist across the table. "You're a cool dude."

Aaron tapped his knuckles against Michael's. "Thanks."

He looked my way again, and I grinned. *Very cool dude!*

"So you should hang with us next Saturday," Michael said. "At the hotel. I'm rooming with Brandon and we're having a party. I figure we'll all need to chill after auditions."

"Yeah, maybe," Aaron said. "Thanks."

Michael juggled a few jelly beans. "I heard you in the practice room the other day. Your solo is tight."

"It's coming," Aaron said.

"More polished than mine."

I nearly choked on a chocolate-covered gummy bear. "What? But you're not doing a solo." I looked at Lori. "You guys are doing a duet, right?"

"Not . . . exactly," she said slowly.

"Didn't you tell her?" Michael asked. I could see his jaw working. I wasn't sure if he was chewing jelly beans, or suddenly mad.

"Tell me what?" I asked.

Lori ran her fingers around the curls by her ear—a sure sign of nervousness. "Mr. Wayne said we couldn't do it."

"What? For real?" I leaned forward, but I felt like jumping out of my skin. "Why didn't you tell me?"

She flashed a look at Michael. I was missing something, but I couldn't figure out what.

"Lori?" I asked.

She looked back at me and said, "I was going to. Mr. Wayne didn't tell me no until last night after the basketball game."

"You could have told me today."

"I was still hoping I could figure something out."

My brain flooded with so many questions; I couldn't think any of it through. Why did Lori have to figure something out? Was Michael mad at Lori? But it wasn't her fault if Mr. Wayne said no.

"What did Mr. Wayne say exactly?" I asked.

"Just that I can be part of two performances, and that's the limit."

"And you're already signed up for a solo," Aaron said, "and the duet with Tay."

"Bingo," Michael said.

He did sound pissed.

"So—" I began. Then I froze, which was weird, because a thought was burning its way around the edges of my brain. It felt like liquid heat filling my head and flashing red behind my eyes. "You *are* still doing the duet with me, right?"

"Of course," Lori said. "I wouldn't do that to you." And then she shot another look at Michael.

"Okay," I said carefully. I knew I should be relieved, but instead, my stomach clenched around this new, unknown worry.

"At least a solo is worth more points," Aaron said to Michael. "So that might be good."

"It would be—if I had time." He flicked a jelly bean across the table and into some bushes.

Lori sighed. "We thought it was all set."

"Instead, I'm starting over again," Michael added.

"Of course, he's freaked." Lori went on. "His dad already booked tickets to come out for the concert."

"My dad bought me a bracelet," I said. "With an engraved charm."

Michael and Lori both gave me long looks.

I turned to Aaron for backup, and he handed me a couple of gummy worms. I took them. Good idea—chew, don't talk.

"If Michael doesn't get in, it's going to be a big deal in his family," Lori said. "I mean, his dad plays professionally."

There was that worried look on Michael's face again. I concentrated on the worm I'd stretched into a shoelace.

"That's tough," Aaron said.

"Things are cool with my dad," Michael said. "It isn't that. I'm going to go live with him in New York—there's a plan all worked out." He lined up another jelly bean and shot it. "But no way I can transfer to NYC and get into a conservatory if I can't prove I'm serious about music." His gaze swept around the table. "My dad is cool with it, but my mom is busting me for proof. That's why I need District Honor Band and Wind Ensemble."

So he can be with his dad. I curved a hand over my stomach, wishing I didn't sympathize.

For a second, there was a long silence, as if no one knew what to say. Then Lori's phone burst into Beethoven. She reached for her purse and dug out her cell. "It's my mom," she said as she answered.

"Hey," she said into the phone, then paused and nodded. "Okay." She tucked her cell away. "She'll be here in five."

"That quick?" Michael swung his legs around the bench.

"It'll take her a few minutes to make it through the traffic," Lori said, standing up. "We'll wait for you by the candy store," she told me. She took Michael's hand, and they disappeared into the crowd.

I let out a long breath. "Wow," I said to Aaron. "Can you believe that? They're not doing a duet, after all." I rested my hands on my cheeks. They felt hot.

"I wonder why Lori didn't tell you?"

"I don't know. She'll fill me in later, I guess." I shook my head. "And what about all that stuff with Michael wanting to move to New York? A *conservatory*?"

"Yeah, well." He shrugged. "We all want to get in, Tay."

I nodded. Aaron was right. But playing in a conservatory sounded so important, and way more impressive than my goal of being a band director one day. I'd never even told anyone, it sounded that stupid. But I'd always thought I'd be a good band director. I'd cry at all our concerts, just like Mr. Wayne.

They're not doing a duet.

The words swirled around my brain again, but this time they actually sank in. A shiver went through me—a good one. One that made the hairs on my arm stand up and do a happy dance.

Maybe I did have a chance. Maybe this was the break I needed. Maybe, if I impressed Hallady during the audition . . . I took a long shuddering breath and said the words out loud that I had hardly dared to think. "Maybe I *can* make Wind Ensemble next year."

"Why not?" Aaron said matter-of-factly.

"Because I'm not freaking good like you are," I said, my hands fisting up in frustration. "I don't pick up new music the way you do, and my fingers move at about half the speed."

"But when you play, it's not just a lot of notes. It

sounds like something. And your technique is getting stronger. Don't shake your head," Aaron said. "I sit next to you, remember? You are good."

I wanted to smack him and hug him, and I wanted to cover my face with my hands and scream. I settled for pressing my shoulder into his. "This whole night . . . it's too much to take it all in. The movie, and the band stuff . . . and the physics stuff!" I grinned up at him. "That totally surprised me."

"I took a class at science camp last summer on the physics of skateboarding."

I shook my head, impressed. "And now Michael's inviting you to his party."

"You have to come, too."

I laughed because the feeling inside me was too big to keep in. "What a totally amazing night."

"Yeah." In the overhead lights, it looked like his eyes were glittering.

"I wish I didn't have to go. You sure you don't need a ride?"

"Yeah, my brother's at the bookstore."

I stood and looked out into the parking lot. "Mrs. Van Sant must be here by now." Then I turned back to say good-bye, and nearly squeaked in surprise. Aaron had stood up so close I could feel his breath on my cheek.

I stepped back. "Thanks again for going along with this."

"Except," he said, "if I were your real boyfriend, I'd kiss you good-bye. Like this."

Before I could think what he meant, he leaned in and kissed me.

On the lips.

♩ 20 ♫

I jerked back. My legs smacked the cement bench, and I stumbled, sitting hard. My heart thundered down to the tips of my fingers. "What was that?"

He stuffed his hands in his pockets. "You couldn't tell?"

I covered my mouth with my fingers. "That wasn't part of the plan."

"Sorry. I decided to improvise."

I stood up, trying to balance. Trying to reboot my brain. My breath raced in and out so fast, I couldn't get any air. "We're friends, Aaron."

"With chemistry."

"With static cling." But it sounded lame to my own ears, especially with my heart pounding hard enough to dent my ribs.

He trailed a hand around the back of his neck, and I could see his breath was shaky, too. "I like you, Tay."

"I like you, too. But . . ."

"But what?" he asked in a low voice. "I'm okay for pretend dates, but not real ones?"

"No!" I said in a rush. "It's not that."

"Then what?"

"I don't know." With shaky fingers, I traced over my lips. *My just-kissed lips!* My head spun like a cotton-candy machine. "I do really like you," I said, struggling to understand it myself. "I just never thought . . ." I swallowed. "I mean . . ." I sat down again, resting my hands on the rough cement to steady myself. "I don't know what I mean. Things are changing too fast."

"Uncertainty Principle," he said as he sat beside me.

"Yeah, well, uncertainty sucks. I want things to stay the way they are."

His hands were still stuffed in his pockets, his shoulders hunched forward. "Not all change has to be bad."

"I know." I paused, searching for words. "But that's how it's been lately. With Lori and Michael. My parents separating. My mom packing heat. Don't ask," I added when he blinked in confusion. "I don't want things to get messed up with you, too."

He dropped a hand to the bench, his fingers resting an inch from mine. "Who says they have to?" One side of his mouth tilted up.

Okay, he is seriously cute.

"They just usually do."

"I'm not asking for a kidney, Tay." He shifted his

hand until his fingers touched mine. "I just want to hang out."

Little tingles shot up my arm from where our fingers touched. Still, I didn't move my hand away.

Aaron likes me? He like-likes *me?*

"You really didn't know?" he asked as if he'd read my mind. "Even after last night? Grabbing your hand like that wasn't exactly smooth."

I blushed. "Considering I'd just asked you out on a fake date, it didn't seem so strange."

The sound of voices filled the air as a crowd of people walked by. I'd almost forgotten we were still sitting outside the movie theater.

"Here's the thing, Tay," he said; then he paused and cleared his throat. "I like being around you. You're funny and talented and smart—when you're not being so clueless."

I attempted an eye-roll, but it's not easy when your cheeks are on fire.

His voice dropped to a near whisper. "I think you're totally and completely cool. And I think we should go out—for real this time."

Me and Aaron—for real. Aaron—but not Aaron. How could he be my same old friend but suddenly make my stomach quiver? I lifted the hair from the back of my neck, wishing for a cool breeze. How would I face him on Monday morning? Would things change in band and in science? I thought about how much I looked forward to our classes together and how he always made me laugh. Would we go back to how we were, or would I hyperventilate every time I saw him?

I stared at where our fingers were still barely touching, my heart settling into a breathless sprint. "What if we do start going out? What happens at school? Will you turn weird?"

"I'm not planning to."

"Because people get weird when they start dating, and they act differently."

"I won't." His fingers snuck closer, sliding over mine. Warmth shot up my arm. "Are you going to text me fifty times a day?"

"Do you want me to?"

"No," I said. "At least, I don't think so."

"Okay." He curled his fingers around mine. "Are you going to want us to wear matching bracelets?"

"No!" Then I thought of the black cord around Lori's wrist. "But what if I did?"

He shrugged. "Then I'd wear one, I guess."

"I'm not letting you win at Sudoku," I said.

"And I'm not going to let you do all the cutting in science lab."

"But I will anyway."

He laughed. "Sounds like the usual."

"I guess so," I admitted.

"Except next time I kiss you, maybe you won't freak out."

"I didn't freak out," I said automatically. But I had. Inside, I didn't even feel like myself. Shaky, but good, too.

"Meet me tomorrow?" he asked. His eyes were the color of melted caramel and just as warm.

"Where?"

"The bookstore. At noon?"

"Okay. If I can."

We both stood, and when he held my hand, my heart turned a cartwheel. We headed to the candy store, and I wondered if other people watched us. I hoped so. This was me, Tatum Austin, holding hands with Aaron Weiss.

Because he thought I was totally and completely cool.

And somewhere deep down, I felt like maybe I actually was.

♪ 21 ♫

The corner of the mattress dipped under the weight of Lori's knees as she rolled across my side of the trundle and onto her bed. In the dark with the blinds closed, the orange walls faded to black and the only light was a tiny glow from the stars stuck on the ceiling.

I curled the covers up over my shoulders and turned to face her. "Was that not the best night—"

"—ever," she finished with a smile.

We'd thrown on our sleep shirts, brushed our teeth in a hurry, and now I was warm under the covers and as happy as I'd been in maybe forever.

"Our first real date," I murmured, letting the words sink in.

"Did you see Alesia and Stace?" Lori asked.

I shook my head.

"They were walking up to the movies when we were. I hope they heard Michael when we first met up."

"You mean when he said you were hot?"

She giggled.

"My jeans looked great on you."

"Can you believe I fit into them?" She sighed. "He actually slid one hand into my back pocket—and there was room."

My heart squeezed, extrahappy for Lori. "You gotta keep them—they look better on you, anyway."

"They do not." But I saw the gleam of her teeth as she smiled. "I'll take them though, if you're sure. They'll be anniversary jeans, because I wore them on our first date." Her smile widened. "We kissed outside the candy store—in front of everyone."

"And while Michael was kissing you, Aaron was kissing me."

We sighed in unison and then laughed.

We lay side by side, near enough that I could see her face but everything else was blanketed by the dark. I loved the feeling—as if it were just the two of us in the world, whispering things no one else could know.

"So what was it like?" she asked. "When he kissed you?"

I brushed the hair off my forehead as I thought back. "Quick," I said.

Lori laughed.

"It was good, though, because then I didn't have time to think about it. I must have closed my eyes, but I'm not sure."

"Isn't it weird?" she said. "I used to worry about

that—would I close my eyes or not? And where would our noses go, and what would I do with my hands? And then it just happens. And you're not thinking about anything."

"I know," I said. "I had this weird flash in my brain that Aaron has freckles—and the next minute he's kissing me, and I'm like, *Aaron?*"

"I know," she said. "You guys have been friends forever."

"Now we're friends who kiss." I touched my lips with my fingers and smiled. "He's not just this smart guy, Lori. He's really cool, you know?"

She nodded. "That physics stuff he went into? That was major. Michael was so impressed."

My smile faded as the rest of our conversation flooded back. "I'm sorry about the duet with Michael. He looked kind of mad about it."

She bunched her pillow up beneath her cheek. "More like really mad."

"At you? Why?"

"Michael and I spent almost a week practicing a duet he can't do. Now he's lost all that time. He thinks I should have checked with Mr. Wayne first, but I never thought he would say no."

"At least you tried."

"Michael doesn't see it that way. That's why I didn't say anything to you yet—I was hoping I could come up with a Plan B." Her voice dipped. "He even got his mom to call Mr. Wayne today, but he won't budge. District rule."

"Wow," I breathed. "His mom called Mr. Wayne at home?"

"Told you he's serious. I mean, you heard him about the music conservatory. Plus, there's his dad. Michael didn't say it in so many words, but I don't think his dad will bother coming out if he doesn't make the Honor Band. He hasn't been to see Michael once in two years." She tapped a fist against her chest. "It just breaks my heart. I want to help him so much. You know how it is. If it were Aaron, you'd want to help him, too."

"Yeah," I said, silently making a vow to be nicer to Michael from now on. *Two years?* "I can totally understand."

Her face lit up. "I knew you could. You're so great about that—you always understand. I told Michael you would."

I frowned, suddenly sensing that she meant something different than I did. "What did you tell Michael?"

"That you'd understand what's at stake." Her eyes blinked at me, wide and intent. "That you'd see the big picture."

"There's a big picture?" I said slowly.

She sat up a little, propping herself on an elbow. "He wants to transfer to New York his junior year and focus on music. He could end up playing with his dad's orchestra."

"I know," I said, my mouth suddenly dry.

"And a lot depends on District Honor Band."

I struggled to swallow. "I feel bad, Lori, I do. Honest. But District Honor Band means a lot to me, too. I have a chance to make Wind Ensemble if I impress Dr. Hallady," I added. "Mr. Wayne thinks I can—I told you that."

"But he's a teacher. He's supposed to say those things."

I didn't have time to hide my face. To pretend her words didn't feel like a slap.

Her expression changed in a heartbeat. Her cheeks reddened as if she were the one just smacked. "Tay, I didn't mean it that way. It came out wrong. I just meant you'd hate Wind Ensemble—you always say Dr. Hallady freaks you out."

I wound my arms around my knees, cold under the blanket. What she really meant was she didn't think I could make it. Which suddenly made me feel stupid for thinking I could. My eyes prickled with tears. I blinked, forcing myself to shrug. If we didn't stop talking about this, I was going to end up crying. "Let's just forget it."

"Tay, no. All I meant was you'll love concert band with Mr. Gibbs. That's why when Michael wanted me to talk to you . . ." She blinked nervously, then shifted onto her back. "Never mind."

The heat behind my eyes burned while more gathered at the back of my throat. "Never mind what?"

"I don't know if I should say it now."

Suddenly, I remembered the weird looks between Lori and Michael tonight. "Say what?"

She turned back toward me and wet her lips nervously. "Michael thought if you understood, maybe you'd help him out with District Honor Band."

I took a breath, but the fresh scent of the sheets had faded. Now the air felt full of something heavy and bad. Which was stupid. Air was just hydrogen and oxygen. "How could I help him out? I'm not Dr. Hallady. I'm not judging."

"But if you didn't have a totally perfect performance . . ."

I gasped, but there was no noise. No air. I felt like I was choking on nothing but the sound of her words.

"Not bad or anything," she said quickly.

"It's part of my grade, Lori."

"You'd still get an A," she said. "You wouldn't bomb it or anything."

"I can't believe you're even asking me this."

She reached out a hand, but I was wrapped too tightly inside the covers for her to find my arm. "I wouldn't if it weren't so important."

"But it's District Honor Band!"

"I know," she said. "That's the worst part. The weekend of the concert won't be any fun without you. But it's only a few days. You said yourself you'd want to help Aaron if you could."

"Yeah, but—"

"I wouldn't ask if there was any other way." Her voice pleaded in the dark. "You don't know what it's been like since Mr. Wayne said no. It's so important to Michael, and I screwed up the whole duet thing. I'm afraid what he'll do if I can't fix it." Her voice shook with tears. "I'm afraid he's going to break up with me."

"So?" I cried. "Why would you want a boyfriend like that?"

"Easy for you to say," she snapped. "You're not Lori 'the size of a van' Sant."

"No one calls you that anymore."

"That doesn't mean I've forgotten what it feels like. With Michael, I'm not that girl. I'm skinny and beautiful, and it's like I've never been anything else. Can't you try and understand what that means to me?"

"I do, but—"

"It's not just that," she went on. "We talk about so many things, and he totally gets me."

"That's great, but—"

"It's not great," she interrupted, tears spilling off her lashes. "Because I'm so afraid I'll wake up one morning and it'll all be gone."

She sobbed the last words, her voice so full of pain the sound of it hurt. I squeezed my eyes shut; I didn't want to hear. I didn't want to care.

What about me?

But it wasn't just me. It was *us*. We'd always gotten

through everything together. Slowly, I untwined my hand from the sheet and reached out to touch her arm.

Lori blinked up at me. Tears had left shiny trails of silvery light on her cheeks. "I'm so sorry, Tay. I don't know what else to do. I can't lose him."

But you can lose me? The thought whispered through my heart before I could stop it. I already knew the answer. She didn't have to worry about losing me—I might be mad, but I'd get over it. I always did.

"I understand, I really do," I said, my voice a thready whisper. "But you can't ask me to do this. Please."

"I won't," she said. "You're right." She wiped her cheeks dry and nodded. "It would only be if you wanted to."

If I wanted to?

"I would never forget it," she added. "Not ever. And I'd make it up to you. I don't know how, but I would. I swear. Because you're the best friend there is. You always come through for me. Always."

She looked at me, pleading, and I thought of all the times I'd looked at her just the same way.

Save me, please.

And she had. From that first day of school when she saved a spot next to her and every day after when I'd known I had a best friend. A friend who liked me as much as I liked her—who liked me better than anyone else.

When I'd been too scared to go off the high dive at Y summer camp, Lori had climbed up and gone off with me, holding my hand, even though it was against the rules. In sixth grade, when I panicked over auditions and couldn't see myself ever performing, she'd brought me a duet and I'd seen my first glimmer of hope. And when Dad and Mom sat us down at the breakfast table to tell Andrew and me about the separation, it was Lori's house I'd run to, gasping and crying. I hadn't been able to take a full breath until it was just the two of us in her rainbow-sherbet room.

And now, she needed *me* to save *her*.

By giving up my dream.

I shifted over so I lay on my back. The stars glowed down at me, though the Milky Way had started peeling off the ceiling. I'd have to fix that tomorrow.

If only I could fix everything else.

"I'm kind of tired," I managed to say through the heavy lump of tears stuck in my throat. "I'm going to go to sleep, okay?"

"Yeah, sure," she said softly.

She reached over and pulled me into a tight hug. "I'm so lucky to have you." Her shirt felt scratchy on my cheek. "Best friends, right?"

I nodded, not trusting myself to say anything. Then I eased away from her and flipped over onto my other side.

I could hear Lori's even breathing behind me. My

eyes burned like they were tired, but I wondered how I could ever fall asleep.

Or maybe I was asleep.

Maybe this was just a bad dream. I tried to remember sitting with Aaron and holding his hand. I tried to remember what Totally and Completely Cool had felt like.

I looked around Lori's room—at the outline of the beanbag chairs and her desk. Her room was almost as familiar as my own. I'd always felt at home here, right from the beginning. So why did I feel so lost?

All of a sudden, I wished I was in my own bed. Tomorrow was Sunday. Sunday mornings at home, we used to get doughnuts and eat them in the family room in our pajamas. I got a chocolate long john with sprinkles, and Andrew got the one with maple frosting, and Dad liked cinnamon twists, and Mom always said none for her, but we'd bring her an apple fritter anyway, and she'd eat every bite.

I squeezed my eyes shut against a wave of tears. I wanted to go back. I wanted to be a kid again. I wanted to hold my dad's coffee cup while he drove us to the store, and I wanted to press my nose to the doughnut case and watch the lady fill our box. I wanted us all to sit together on a big blanket in the family room and have Mom tease me for getting frosting in my hair. I wanted to laugh at Dad and Andrew arguing over the sports page while they shared the same glass of milk.

I wanted to go back to before Michael Malone moved here, before I'd stopped wanting doughnuts because Lori said they had too many calories. Back to before Mom dressed up in hairnets and Dad lived somewhere else. Before things had gotten so complicated.

Back to when it had been enough just to be part of Tay-Lo.

♪ 22 ♫

I found Aaron between mystery and science fiction. He sat in a plaid purple armchair, his hair shaggy and covering his eyes again, an oversized book across his lap.

"Hey," I said, dropping into the chair next to him.

He looked up and broke into a huge smile. "Hey."

No guy had ever smiled at me like that. Make that no human being. For the first time all day, I felt like smiling back.

I crossed a foot over my knee, running a hand around the toe of my sneaker where Lori and I had drawn hearts and stars in red Sharpie. I'd felt a little nervous on the drive over—I'd never met my boyfriend at the bookstore before. I'd never had a boyfriend to meet. Then again, it was just Aaron.

The Aaron who'd kissed me last night.

Butterflies whipped around my stomach every time

I thought about it. And I'd already thought about it a million times this morning. For one thing, it was way better than thinking about Lori.

He pointed toward the self-help section. "Who is that?"

I looked over and groaned silently. "That's my mom. Ignore her."

She'd driven me here and promised not to bother us. I should have made her promise not to stalk invisible enemies in the aisles. I covered my face with a hand and cringed through the gap in my fingers. That's what she was doing, her knees bent as she crept around a shelf of self-help books, popping her head up every few seconds to look toward the door.

"Does she have bad knees?"

"She's pretending to be a secret agent nurse," I said, "for the play she's in."

He studied my mom with new interest. "That explains the shoes."

I groaned again, this time out loud. I'd told her not to wear the rubbery white shoes. "At least the bookstore is carpeted," I said. "On tile floors, it sounds like she's walking on bags of potato chips."

"She has to wear them in public?"

"Her director wants her to develop a character walk. It was her idea to wear them twenty-four-seven. She's also taken to wearing basketball nets on her head."

He grinned. "She looks like she's having fun."

I turned toward my mom again, trying to see her as Aaron did. Other than the crab-walk and nurse shoes, she looked like anybody else, I guessed. Come to think of it, her eyes didn't have that tired red look today. And she'd been smiling when she picked me up from Lori's house. I'd asked about the acting exercise last night. She said they'd gotten strange looks at Denny's (*what a shock!*), but she'd had fun.

Fun?

"She does seem okay, doesn't she?" I said slowly. "Maybe she's in denial."

"Is she working things out with your dad?"

"I don't think so," I admitted. "They hardly see each other, and all I ever hear them talk about is Andrew and me. Besides, it's not like Dad's going to swoon at her feet if she's wearing those shoes."

"Yeah, but guys love the basketball-net look."

I couldn't help but smile. "You're an idiot."

"And you have a thing for idiots?"

I laughed. "Looks that way." I pointed to his book. "So what are you reading?"

"A book on stars. Figured I'd better read up so I know what you're talking about." He leaned toward my chair. "Astronomy is pretty cool." He pointed to a picture that looked like a red firecracker across a black sky. "When big stars die, they explode."

"That's what's cool? Dying stars?"

"Exploding stars." He grinned. "I googled the hotel

for Saturday night. It's next to a desert preserve, so I bet we'll see a ton of stars."

I nodded, but the butterflies flapped in my stomach again. This time, in a bad way. Saturday night reminded me of Saturday. And auditions. And Lori asking me to screw up so Michael could make it ahead of me.

"What is it?" Aaron asked. "You just turned three shades whiter."

"It's something that happened last night." I tugged on my ponytail, tightening it. "With Lori."

He shook back his hair, his expression wary. "And?"

"She brought up Michael again. She says it's really important for him to make District Honor Band."

"So you told her it's important for you, too, right?"

"A few months ago I wasn't even going to try for Wind Ensemble."

"But you are now."

"Lori doesn't think I have a chance."

"What?" The book almost fell off his lap. "She said that?"

"Not in so many words." I dropped my head against the chair cushion. I'd hardly slept all night, and my head ached. "Maybe she's right. Maybe I've just been stupid about all of this."

"About what?"

"About thinking I'm better than I am."

He set down the open book, shaking his head the whole time. "Okay, now you are being stupid. Who cares what Lori thinks?"

"She only said what I was half thinking myself. Maybe it wouldn't be such a bad thing if Michael got the spot."

"What?" He stared at me like I had a hole in my head. Maybe I did. It was pounding bad enough.

"It would mean a lot to Lori."

"So?"

"I wouldn't even have made District Honor Band last year if not for her."

"You don't know that."

"She's always been there for me, Aaron. When my parents split, I practically lived at her house."

"So?" he snapped again.

"So, this is really important to her, and I can do something about it."

"Do what?"

A lump rose in my throat and I swallowed hard. "I can let Michael win."

His jaw dropped. "You're kidding me, right?"

"It's not like I want to."

"Then don't!"

I pressed a hand to my throbbing temple. "She's my best friend. If I don't do it, she'll say District Honor Band means more than she does."

"So?"

"Would you stop saying that!" I cried. "Friends make sacrifices for each other. You just don't understand."

His eyes narrowed, the dark rim of his irises looking almost black. "You think I don't understand? I sat in the second row all year just to be by you."

"What?" I shook my head, hardly able to make sense of it. "You did what?"

"I should be sitting first row, probably first chair. But I told Mr. Wayne not to move me up."

"But . . . For me?"

"Why do you always sound so shocked?" He rolled his eyes. "Yeah, for you. Maybe it was stupid, but I was only screwing up myself. What Lori is asking . . . that's messed up."

"She's desperate," I said.

"You kidding me? You're going to defend her? Do you even see what's happening?"

"Yeah, I see." Tears squeezed out of my eyes. Didn't Aaron see he was making it all worse?

Instead, he leaned closer, his voice like sandpaper on my nerves. "She's using you, and you're letting her."

"I am not."

"It's beyond lame."

His words stung and anger filled me. "If that's what you think, then why are we even going out?"

His head jerked back like I'd hit him.

I covered my mouth with a hand, as if I could hold back the words that had already escaped. "I'm sorry. I didn't mean that. Let's not fight, okay?"

"Then what should we do?" he growled. "Or do you want to ask Lori what she thinks?"

"Stop it, Aaron, please!"

He reached for the star book, flipped some pages, and then shoved it onto my lap.

"You want to know something else I just read?" He stabbed at the page with a finger. "Some of the stars you see in the sky right now are dead. They've been dead for years. You're looking at something that's not even there anymore. That's your friendship with Lori.

He stood up, turning his back to me. "I'm out of here."

I watched him stride away. *He'd given up first part to sit by me?* Good thing I was so numb. Or I had a feeling that would hurt more than I could handle.

Silently, tears dripped onto the book. It looked as if even the stars were crying.

♪ 23 ♫

Begin whenever you're ready." Mr. Wayne crossed his hands over his wide middle and leaned back in the chair. His office smelled like coffee and mints. Usually, it was a good smell, but today my stomach gurgled as if I had a leaky pipe inside me.

I glanced at Lori, who sat beside me, and pressed a hand over my belly. Maybe it was something I'd eaten. Only I hadn't been able to eat much for the last few days.

Today was Wednesday, our final play-through for Mr. Wayne. Only three more days until auditions and our night at the hotel. I'd looked forward to it for so long.

Now I dreaded it.

Outside Mr. Wayne's office, Brandon paced back and forth, waiting to do his solo. Mr. Wayne had scheduled us for fifteen-minute slots. By now we were supposed to have our pieces down.

"You ready?" Lori asked softly. I could tell she was worried, but was she worried about me? Or Michael?

No, I'm not ready. I had a dry reed, a dry mouth, and sweaty palms. But I nodded. She counted off the beat, and I took a breath.

Two measures in, I squealed like a pig on its way to becoming bacon. My cheeks flushed hot. I stopped and wiggled my ligature. "My reed wasn't on straight," I lied.

Lori counted off the beat again, and this time I squealed on the third note.

Lori shot me a look. I shot her one back.

I could just guess what she was thinking. *Don't mess up yet, Tay. Wait for Saturday and your audition with Dr. Hallady—when it really counts.*

I blinked, waiting for the music to come back into focus. She counted off the beat a third time. I took a breath—

And squealed on the opening note.

"Sorry," I muttered.

"Is there a problem with your instrument?" Mr. Wayne asked.

I shook my head, too miserable to say a word. Mr. Wayne hadn't brought up the solo again—even he'd realized I was totally hopeless.

Like Aaron had.

I didn't want to think about Aaron. I used to ignore

him without even trying to, but now he was permanently stuck in my head. I thought I could fix things, but he wouldn't let me. In science on Monday, I'd made jokes about Sam the frog and let him do all the cutting. He froze me out anyway, until I got mad and threatened him with a straight pin covered in frog skin.

"What do you want me to say?" he had asked.

"I don't know," I said. "Aren't we even friends anymore?"

"Are we?" He had looked at me with eyes as flat and cold as Sam's skin. "Did you check with Lori? Is it okay with her? I wouldn't want you to get in trouble."

Maybe I should have known then. Maybe I should have seen it coming. But I had to choke back a cry when he walked into band on Monday and sat down. In the first row. In a chair that hadn't been there the week before. Even then, I had to hear it from Mr. Wayne.

"We'll be doing a little rearranging in the clarinet section," he told the band. "Aaron will be playing first part. It's so close to the end of the year, I don't want to make any other moves, so we'll just add a chair to the end of the row as we've already done."

Mr. Wayne met my eyes. "Tatum, you can move up one chair, and now you'll be sharing a stand with Michael."

I understood then. Aaron wasn't just moving up. He was breaking up.

As I slid over to the chair that should have been

Aaron's, I hated him. I hated Michael, and I hated Lori, and I wanted to scream out loud that I hated everyone. I wanted to scream that I hated myself.

But I didn't scream. I swallowed back my tears, because that's what I always did. I'd swallowed my hurt when Lori told me about the duet with Michael. I'd swallowed my anger when she asked me to mess up. I'd swallowed my misery over Aaron.

And now, sitting next to Lori in Mr. Wayne's office, all I had to do was swallow my pride. Except...I couldn't. It was too much, all of it swirling around inside me. My stomach shuddered, and the feelings I'd kept inside rose up in a hot, burning ache.

Oh God. I'm going to be sick.

I lurched out of my chair and grabbed the plastic garbage can by Mr. Wayne's desk. I leaned over it just in time. Watery acid came up in waves, like sobs I couldn't control. My hands clenched the sides of the can, until finally, I sank to my knees, empty and exhausted. I squeezed tears from the corners of my eyes and wiped a hand over my mouth.

And suddenly I flashed back to the day in third grade when I'd gotten sick on Lori and unexpectedly discovered my best friend. Here I was again, but had the opposite happened? Had I just lost my best friend?

That heavy girl with the friendly eyes and pink sandals had reshaped herself into someone new. I'd watched it happen . . . watched her discover new things that didn't include me. Was I just being blind like Aaron said? I'd been trying so hard to hold on—but to what?

"I can't do this," I whimpered. "I can't."

Even I wasn't sure who I was talking to. Mr. Wayne— or Lori.

♪ 24 ♫

Sounds like stomach flu," I heard the nurse say through the open door. "She was sick in Phillip Wayne's office."

"Where is she?" a worried voice asked. My mom.

"Lying down on one of the beds."

"Thanks, Janet."

Janet was Mrs. Garcia, the school nurse, and I'd told her not to call Mom. I'd told her she'd be teaching, and I'd just wait for school to be over.

I lay back, resting my head against the wall, and listened to Mom's quick strides down the short hall. For some reason, just hearing her footsteps made me want to cry.

The door creaked open a few more inches. Mom saw me and smiled. "Hi, honey," she said as she closed the door behind her.

She looked weird in this white room. Too colorful. She wore a yellow shirt, purple skirt, and black polka-dot tennis shoes. Sometimes her teacher outfits made me want to cringe, but today she just looked good.

"You okay?" She brushed aside a few loose strands of my bangs and laid her hand on my forehead. "No fever."

"It's just my stomach. I told Mrs. Garcia not to call."

She sat beside me, barely fitting both legs next to mine. It wasn't much of a bed. Thin mattress, scratchy sheet, lumpy pillow—and a wide strip of blue paper that covered the bottom half. It crinkled as Mom crossed her ankles.

"The kids are all at an assembly this afternoon," she said. "You picked the perfect day to get sick."

She smiled and I did, too. Only my smile wobbled, and all of a sudden tears were rolling down my cheeks like rain.

Mom didn't say anything, just leaned her head back against the wall and waited. Her hand curved around mine, and I held on, crying silently in case someone out there was listening.

When my shoulders stopped shaking, she handed me a tissue. That was a good thing about kindergarten teachers. They always had tissues in their pockets.

I let go of her hand and blew my nose.

"It's not really the stomach flu, is it?" she asked softly.

I shook my head.

She shifted just enough to study my face as if she were reading me like a book. Talk about a horror story.

"You haven't been yourself since you came home from Lori's the other morning," she said. "You ready to tell me why?"

"I can't. It sounds so bad."

She reached for my hand again. "It's okay. Moms can handle anything."

"It's about District Honor Band." I sniffled and took a long breath. "Lori tried to help Michael by doing a duet with him, too, only then Mr. Wayne said she couldn't."

"Because she's doing one with you?" Mom asked.

I nodded. "Michael got mad because now he has to do a solo. And Lori's afraid Michael will break up with her because of it. She asked me if I'd help."

The strip of paper crinkled as Mom shifted again. "How could you help?"

"By having a bad audition."

Her eyebrows shot up. "She asked you to play badly on purpose?"

"Only if I want to," I whispered.

"Why in the world would you want to?" she exclaimed.

"For our friendship." I pulled my hand free and twisted the tissue in my fingers. "I told you it sounds bad. Aaron called me lame when I told him. And then he broke up with me." I shrugged helplessly as new tears gathered. "I didn't know what to do. Today, I tried to play for Mr. Wayne, and I couldn't stop squeaking. I felt so sick that I threw up in his office."

"Heavens," Mom muttered. She handed me a new tissue. "Why didn't you just tell Lori no?"

"I wanted to," I said, "but Lori's my best friend. She's been there for me—and I figured that I should be there for her."

"What about being there for yourself?" Mom said stiffly.

I swallowed a sob. My throat still ached from being sick. "I wish Michael had never moved here."

"Don't blame this on Michael," she snapped. "It's not Michael's fault. It's not even Lori's fault. Yes, I'm disappointed that she would ever ask you to play poorly. But more than that, I'm disappointed that you would even consider it."

The bite in Mom's voice stung. "I didn't know what else to do."

"How about coming right out and flatly telling her no?"

"I tried," I groaned. "But it would have turned into a fight."

"So? You've had fights before."

"It's different this time."

"Because of Michael?"

"Because of everything." I threw up a hand, the wet tissue wadded in my fist. "Because she's beautiful and thin and she has a boyfriend and she could have other friends if she wants."

"Ah," Mom said, nodding her head slowly. "So she won't need you. Is that it?"

"Maybe," I muttered, but the new stream of tears said *yes*.

"Oh, Tatum," she said with a sigh. "I'm sorry I didn't see what was happening before now. Of course things are changing for Lori."

"But why does that mean *we* have to change?"

She rubbed my back softly. "It's just usually how it goes. But if Lori is a friend worth keeping, you'll work things out."

"That's what I was trying to do," I said. "Work things out."

"By giving up your dream for hers?" Mom shook her head. "No friend would want that."

"You don't get it," I mumbled.

She raised my chin until our eyes met. "You don't think I understand about being suddenly alone? About losing a person you've relied on for years?"

My heart thudded at the look in her eyes. "You mean Dad?"

She nodded.

"But you're going to get back together." I twisted the tissue until it shredded in my hand. "Aren't you?"

"No, honey," she said. "We aren't. Your father and I . . ." She took a breath.

"You miss him," I blurted, before she could say anything else. "I know you do."

She slid up straighter, stretching the paper under her shoes until it ripped in a jagged line. "I'm sad, Tatum. I've been sad because I love your dad in many ways. And your dad loves me, too, which makes this so hard. But we don't love each other anymore in the way that married people should. And yes, being alone after nineteen years of marriage is hard. It'll be hard for a long while, I guess." Her fingers feathered over my cheek. "For all of us, I know. And I'm sorry for that. But you know we love you and that hasn't changed."

She sighed. "I understand how you feel about Lori. How scary it is to think about losing a person you've relied on. But the amazing thing about standing on your own two feet—you find your balance. And you get stronger with each passing day."

"It won't be like that for me. I'm not—"

She put her fingers to my mouth, stopping my words. "Don't tell me who you aren't, Tay. Tell me who you are."

She dropped her hand, and I opened my mouth again. But my throat was empty of words.

"Tell me who Tatum Austin is," Mom urged. "In your own words."

I licked my lips. "A good friend."

"Okay," she said with a nod. "What else?"

I leaned back against the wall. "Aaron thinks I'm funny."

"I want to know what *you* think."

"I guess I'm funny," I said. "And I'm good at numbers. And Mr. Wayne says—" I stopped myself. "I have nice clarinet tone when there's no spit in my mouthpiece."

Mom smiled and patted my hand. "Is it so hard to recognize that you're a talented and special person? We all see it, Tay. Me. Your dad. Mr. Wayne. But it doesn't matter what we think. It matters what *you* think."

She slid her arm over my shoulders, pulling me closer. "Can I give you a piece of mom advice?"

"Can I stop you?"

"No." I felt her smile against my cheek, and then she said, "It's okay to be afraid. Everyone is afraid in their own way. The trick is to not let that fear stop you from doing what you want. So tell me this—what do you really want? Is it District Honor Band?"

I didn't even have to think. "Yeah. I want to make District Honor Band, and I know it could help me make Wind Ensemble. I really want that, too, but—"

"No buts," she interrupted. "And how does Lori fit in to that?"

I took a long breath. "She's still my best friend."

"Then she'll support you, Tatum. You just need to be honest with her. Can you do that?"

I blew my nose again and nodded slowly.

"Good," she said, giving my shoulder a squeeze. "So

what can you do to give yourself the best possible chance of making District Honor Band?"

"I probably should have played a solo," I said. "But it's too late now. Auditions are only three days away."

"So?" she said, raising one eyebrow.

"I can't pull together a solo in three days."

"Who says you can't?" she challenged. "'Can't' is what we tell ourselves when something is hard. But, in fact, you *can*."

"But I wouldn't do very well."

"Are you doing well with your duet?"

I paused a second. "No."

"Well, then?"

I shook my head. "Lori would kill me for changing at the last minute."

"This isn't about Lori."

"But I've never auditioned by myself before, and Mr. Wayne would have to change the schedule—if he'd even let me, which I bet he wouldn't. It's not worth fighting over."

"This isn't just about District Honor Band," she said. "Don't you see, Tatum? You're fighting for yourself."

That night, I sat on my bed with my soft mattress and my fluffy comforter and my double-stuffed pillow. My Spanish book was open on my lap, but I couldn't concentrate. I might as well have been back in the nurse's office with the smell of antiseptic and the crinkle of protective paper. My brain felt like it was still there . . . still stuck in the middle of a conversation and trying to find a way out.

Lori had called, but I had Mom tell her I was sick. If only it were stomach flu, I could work through it and be back to normal in three days. But I didn't think I was going to be back to normal after this. I didn't think I wanted to be.

What do you really want?

My mom's words kept repeating themselves in my head. What I wanted was to kick butt at my audition and make District Honor Band. I wanted to tell Lori what I really felt and not worry that she'd stop being my friend. I wanted to be the person everyone else saw in me.

A girl who was funny and smart and a good clarinet player.

A girl who was totally and completely cool.

I glanced over at my backpack. It lay against the wall, the zipper still open and folders hanging halfway out. The blue folder had all of my band music, my duet with Lori—and the solo Mr. Wayne had given me. But I couldn't do a solo. I couldn't— I stopped myself the way Mom had stopped me earlier.

Okay, so actually, I could do a solo. There was nothing that said I couldn't. I dropped the Spanish book on my bed and hopped off before I could chicken out. I jogged to the top of the stairs and called down.

"Mom, can I get a ride to school early tomorrow? There's something I want to talk to Mr. Wayne about."

♪ 25 ♫

They were waiting when I got there. Mr. Wayne sat at his desk, his clipboard in one hand and a cup of coffee in the other. Lori had set up chairs and the music stand. Her flute was already put together and resting on her lap.

"Hey," she said, giving me a long look.

I smiled at her, but I didn't exactly meet her eyes.

"I trust you're feeling better, Miss Austin?" Mr. Wayne asked.

I wasn't feeling too fantastic, but at least I didn't want to puke. For now.

"Sorry about yesterday," I said. I sniffed hesitantly, but thankfully it didn't smell like throw-up in his office.

"Where's your clarinet?" Lori asked.

I lowered my backpack to the carpet. I'd texted her to come early, and I knew she thought we were meeting to finish our play-through. Mr. Wayne probably did, too.

The clock above his desk ticked like a metronome. Twenty minutes until first period. Was that long enough to fix this?

Or ruin everything?

"I didn't bring my clarinet." I finally raised my eyes to the best friend I'd ever had in my life. "I decided not to do our duet."

"What?" Her blue eyes blinked wide, but I could almost see the thoughts chasing themselves through her mind. She half turned so Mr. Wayne couldn't see the look she shot me. "Of course we're going to do the duet. You still need to get your A."

"I will," I said, sounding more confident than I felt.

I turned to Mr. Wayne. "If it's okay, I'd like to do the solo instead. The one you gave me."

"A solo?" Lori repeated.

Mr. Wayne smiled. "You've left it a bit late, Miss Austin, but I applaud your decision. Have you been working on the piece?"

"A little."

"You've been working on a solo?" Lori shot up, nearly knocking over her chair. "Wait a minute. Why didn't you say something before?" She looked at Mr. Wayne. "Does that mean I can do the duet with Michael?"

"With two days until auditions?" He shook his head. "No, Miss Van Sant."

"But you're letting Tay switch!"

"Because Tatum and I have discussed this before." He set down his coffee and stood. "In fact, if you ladies will excuse me, I need to change the schedule. I believe I can still catch the secretary before she makes copies." He swung out of the room at a near jog, his coffee still sloshing in his cup.

It would be cold in a minute the way the temperature in the room had just dropped.

Lori's eyes shot darts of ice. "What is going on?"

I took a breath. *How can you stand on your own two feet when your knees are wobbling?* "I decided to do a solo."

She planted her hands on her hips. "Yeah, I got that. I want to know why. I thought we'd agreed."

I sat in Mr. Wayne's chair, still feeling off balance. "I can't do it, Lori. I'm sorry, but I can't mess up on purpose."

"So instead you're doing a solo? That's messing up even more, if you ask me."

"Not if I play well."

She looked at me in disbelief. "You hate playing alone. You freeze up—you always have. That's why we started doing duets—remember?"

"Yeah, I remember. But I never gave myself a chance. You came up with the idea of a duet, and after that I never even tried a solo."

"Oh, so now it's my fault for not letting you screw up with a solo?"

"I didn't say that." I puffed out a breath of frustration. "I just meant that I might be okay . . . if I let myself try."

"I don't get it." She shoved her hands through her hair. "Did someone talk you into this? Mr. Wayne? Aaron?"

"I decided on my own."

"To do a *solo*?"

She rolled her eyes, and I knew she didn't believe me. It was hard to blame her. I wouldn't have believed me, either.

"If it's because of what I asked you to do, then you should have just said no. I would've understood."

"Does that mean you understand now?" I asked hopefully.

"No," she said, throwing her hands in the air. "You can't just change everything last-minute." Her eyes suddenly widened. "Unless. Was this your plan all along? Work up a solo in secret to get the edge?"

The thought of it was so insane, I actually laughed. "Lori, no."

"Oh, so it's funny now? Ha-ha, joke's on Lori. Is that it? Is this your way of getting back at me for trying to do a duet with Michael?"

"No!" I stood up, holding tight to Mr. Wayne's desk. "It doesn't have anything to do with you—or Michael." I tapped my chest. "It's me, Lori. I should have been doing a solo all along. If I want to be serious about music, I have to get over my fear. You of all people should under-stand."

"What about Michael?" she asked. "He's going to be so pissed."

And in the instant it took for her words to sink in, *I* was pissed. Hadn't she heard me at all? I'd finally spoken up, and it was like I'd said nothing. "Then tell Michael to get over it," I snapped. "You're not in the middle of this anymore, and it has nothing to do with you."

"He'll still blame me," she said, her eyes suddenly shiny with tears.

I let out a growl of frustration. "Why?"

"Because I told him you'd do it."

"You told him—" But I couldn't say another word or I'd scream. I swear I'd scream loud enough to bring Mr. Wayne sprinting from the office.

She held her palms up helplessly. "I thought you would," she said. "Now what do I do?"

"What do *you* do?" My voice crackled I was so hot. "Jeez, Lori. Is that all you can think about? You and Michael?"

She blinked, seemed to get herself under control again. "Sorry. You're right. If you want to do your best, I understand. I'd feel the same way. So we'll just go back to how it was. You'll do your duet like we planned. Michael can do his solo. Whoever gets in, gets in. At least that way Michael won't think this was my idea."

"I can't go back," I said. "I already told Mr. Wayne."

"So untell him."

"I don't want to."

Her eyes widened with hurt. "That's it? No? Doesn't our friendship mean anything to you?"

"Doesn't it mean anything to you?"

She breathed in, and I heard the tremble. If only she'd be okay with this . . . But then her chin lifted, and with it, my heart sank.

"I'm not the one doing this," she said coldly. "You want to do a solo, be my guest. Go solo for the whole weekend for all I care. Go solo *forever*."

"Come on," I said, my voice shaking. "You don't mean that."

"Oh yeah, I do. If this is who you are, then we can't be friends. This, the way you're acting, it's not the Tay I know."

Maybe not, I thought. Maybe I was finally changing, too. Still, my throat closed with fear at the thought of losing my best friend.

Everyone is scared. That's what Mom had said. But that's not how it felt. It felt like I was the only one with weak knees and a spine of pudding. I wanted to be fearless, but I couldn't help it—maybe I'd always be afraid.

But that didn't mean I had to back down. Not now. Not ever again.

"Okay," I told Lori. "I'll see if I can share a room with Kerry and Misa."

Shock flashed in her eyes. Her mouth dropped open but not a sound escaped, as if her voice had frozen along with the rest of her. Then she grabbed her flute and backpack.

"Hope you're happy," she said. And she walked out.

I'd just called in the Winds of Change and blown off the best friend I'd ever had. *Happy?* Not hardly. But I was still standing.

"You need anything?" Dad asked.

I looked up in the middle of a breath, then lowered my clarinet. "Don't you knock?"

"I did," he said. "You didn't hear me. You've been in this closet for so long, I thought you might be thirsty." He held up a bottle of water.

I reached out a hand. "Thanks." The plastic was cold and slick.

"The solo sounds good," he said. "From what I can hear through the door."

I unscrewed the cap and took a long drink. "It's getting better."

"Can I stay and hear you play it all the way through?"

"No." I set the bottle down at my feet.

"Okay. You're the boss." The wrinkles around his eyes deepened as he smiled. "I'm proud of you, Taters."

"I haven't made it yet, Dad."

"It doesn't matter if you do or you don't. I'm proud of you for trying."

I rolled my eyes. "That's one of the annoying things about you and Mom splitting up."

"What?"

"I have to hear the exact same things in two different houses."

He laughed. "I'm glad you wanted to come tonight."

"I'm not sleeping over."

"I know," he said quickly, holding up his hands. "But you're here now, and I was thinking we could do a night hike a little later. We haven't taken the telescope out in a while."

I pointed to the music stand. "I have to practice, Dad. And I can't be up late—I need a good night's sleep. Auditions are tomorrow."

"Right." He nodded seriously. "So I'll just leave you alone." But it sounded like a question. "You might want to practice in front of an audience—"

"Good-bye, Dad," I said.

He grinned and backed out. Before the door closed all the way, I called out, "Dad?"

He peeked his head in. "Yeah?"

"A night hike would be cool, though."

"Next week?" he asked.

I nodded. "Next week."

"My hiking boots are ready whenever you are." He winked and closed the door softly behind him.

The walls creaked, and I could hear my dad's footsteps fading down the stairs. I breathed in the musty warmth of the air mixed with the woodsy smell of my clarinet and reed. I wasn't sure how, but it was starting to feel like home.

I rubbed my sore lips and began again.

♪ 26 ♫

One foot in front of the other.

Mom liked to say that was all you could do sometimes. Put one foot in front of the other and eventually you'd come out the other side.

Eventually? What was that supposed to mean? Math problems did not end in the word "eventually." As in, $A^2 + B^2 = C^2$ *eventually.*

I wanted to know exactly when I'd feel okay again. When I'd stop reaching for my phone to call Lori before I remembered that we weren't talking. When I would crack a smile and not have to think about making it look real.

Most of all, when would this awful day end?

And it had only just begun.

Today was Saturday—District Honor Band auditions and Band Night Out. Early this morning, Mom had dropped me off at the Sunfire Hotel. It wasn't one of those splashy new hotels, but I liked how the adobe buildings felt like part of the desert. Two tall Saguaro cacti towered over the entrance, and inside the lobby, it felt like an old Spanish village. A sign stood by the registration desk welcoming Dakota band members and directing us to the Conference Center for auditions.

Officially, I hadn't switched out of my room with Lori. I didn't want to explain things to Mr. Wayne, and I guess Lori didn't, either. So when I checked in, the desk clerk handed me a key to room 307—the room we would have shared. I stuck it in my bag, and headed to Kerry and Misa's room. They'd been great about letting me share with them.

"Not that you'll stay," Misa had said.

"You'll fix things with Lori before the night is over," Kerry added.

"Why do you say it like that?" I had asked, a little annoyed. "That *I'll* fix things."

"Because you always do," Kerry said with so much certainty I half expected her to offer me a money-back guarantee.

When I knocked on the room door, Kerry flung it open, the inrush of air fluttering the hem of her black dress. "Don't talk to me," she said. "I'm too stressed. I'm going to find a practice room."

She took her sax case and left a minute later. Misa was going to get ready at home, and we'd see her this afternoon.

I did a thirty-second tour of the room. Not bad.

Purple comforters, piles of pillows, and a big TV above a counter with drawers. From the window, I could see the parking lot, but also some of the surrounding desert. I wondered if Lori was in room 307 by now. Was she looking out the window, too? Was she wanting to fix things, or was she waiting for me to fix them like Kerry had said?

I took a deep breath, dumped my overnight bag on the bed, and got busy.

Twenty minutes later, I'd slipped on my audition dress—a black V-neck that swirled around my ankles as I walked. I'd gathered my hair into a pony, then pinned it flat into a bun. I had enough bobby pins jammed into my scalp that if I connected them end-to-end, I'd have a jump rope. For two. Still, I studied myself in the mirror and smiled. I could pass for a concert-band diva.

Now, I just had to play like one.

There were practice areas for warm-up, but I stayed in the room and ran through my scales. My lips were still puffy from so many hours of practice, and my right thumb ached from holding up two pounds of clarinet. Finally, it was time to go. I just had to get through the piece one more time. For Dr. Hallady.

Dad said to embrace my nerves—that the adrenaline would give me a boost. Either that or a heart attack—which was feeling pretty possible as I headed to the audition room. Sweat popped out on my forehead, and my breath sounded like a horror-movie sound track.

Outside, the day was bright and sunny, but in here, the hallway was long and lit only by yellowish overhead lights. The air smelled like it had been recirculated so many times the oxygen had gone out of it. Maybe that's why I couldn't get a full breath.

Behind one of the closed doors, I could make out the sounds of a trombone playing. Dr. Hallady would audition all the wind players while someone else did the percussion and the brass. They had it worked out down to the minute. And I was running out of them.

One foot in front of the other.

It's not easy to drag your feet in heels, but I managed. Maybe I could snag my shoe on a loose carpet thread and suffer a concussion? Then I could spend a relaxing night in the hospital.

It sure beat this.

Lori and I hadn't talked since Thursday. We couldn't exactly avoid each other, since we still sat together in English and I saw her in band every afternoon, but we pretended not to notice each other. Lunch was worse. I'd skipped the cafeteria Thursday and Friday, using the excuse of needing to practice. But what would I do next week when auditions were over?

When auditions were over. By tomorrow morning, we'd know who made it. Then what? Would Lori want to be friends again if I got in? Or only if Michael did? I wondered if things would ever go back to normal. I squinted, trying to picture it in my mind, but I couldn't. As if "normal" was a place that didn't exist anymore.

Kind of like Aaron and me.

Aaron. Even thinking his name hurt. He seemed thrilled with his new seat in band. Steph, our oboe player, sat to the left of Aaron now, and I'd noticed how her chair kept inching closer to his each day. Then yesterday, he'd put Sudoku up on his stand, and she'd giggled like a hyena.

That stung. Less than a week since our date—*our kiss*—and he was playing Sudoku with Steph. Deep down, I couldn't even be mad at him. Not really. I'd pretty much acted like an idiot. Still, I thought he'd say something about my doing a solo. He had to know with the audition schedule posted on Mr. Wayne's door.

I shook my head, trying to clear my brain of all that. I wasn't doing this for Aaron. I was doing this for me.

I looked up, shocked to see room 105 dead ahead. A second later, the door slid open with a soft *whoosh*. Brooke came out, her cheeks flushed and her short hair sticking up as if she'd run her hands through it. As soon as she saw me, she let out an exaggerated silent breath.

"Thank God that's over," she whispered. She stuck her thumb up. "Good luck."

Then she pulled off her spiky-heeled pumps and ran back down the hall, her dress billowing up around her knees.

I had the incredible urge to run with her.

Instead, I gulped in some air and pushed open the door. It was a small conference room, dark and cold, with a long table, a bunch of chairs, and a whiteboard on the back wall. When I stepped in, Dr. Hallady looked up for a second from a chair at the far end. He was writing notes on a clipboard.

"A moment, if you please," he said.

His deep voice never varied from a bored monotone. He wore a black suit with a white shirt that matched his skin. Even with his face tilted down, he kept his mouth pursed. As if he was ready to be disappointed.

Finally, he looked up. His eyes were dark ovals under bushy eyebrows. "And you are?"

"Tatum Austin." If my heart had been a metronome, it would be beating allegretto. Too fast. Way too fast.

"And your piece?"

"Clarinet Concerto by Mozart, second movement," I said, setting my music on the stand.

He draped one thin leg over the other and balanced his clipboard on a knee. "You may begin when you're ready."

I blew out a practice note and then wet my reed again. It sounded so fuzzy. I glanced at Dr. Hallady, then wished I hadn't. He looked so . . . impatient.

"If you get nervous," Mom had said, "visualize Dr. Hallady wearing footie pajamas with bunnies on them. It'll help you remember that he's just a man like any other."

Except there was a good chance that Dr. Hallady wasn't human. Did vampires wear footie pajamas? And why was I thinking about sleepwear for vampires a second before I started my audition?

Panic rose like a lump in my throat. I had a sudden flash of an image: Me. Running. Away. I even reached for my music, but I bumped the stand and it wobbled. I grabbed it and righted it. Somehow, that made me feel better. I might be just as wobbly as the stand, but I was still on my feet, wasn't I?

I thought back to the first time I'd played this piece in Dad's closet. There'd been no one but the shadows to listen. I looked at Dr. Hallady again. I'd gone through so much to get here—and why? For him? For his puckered face and his clipboard? I wasn't going to let him scare me now. I'd play for myself, to prove I could do it, and Dr. Hallady could turn into a bat and fly away for all I cared.

I visualized myself sitting on an old camp chair in a warm, dark closet. I took a deep breath and began.

♪ 27 ♫

The cool thing about auditioning at a hotel with the whole band was that when you kicked butt, you could find someone to brag to around every corner.

The lousy thing was if you'd totally sucked wind, it was almost impossible to hide. I fled down three halls before I found an empty room with the door unlocked.

Not that I'd sucked wind.

Not *totally.*

I ducked into the room and looked around. Four cushioned chairs circled a round table. Along the back wall stood a bar area with a minifridge and coffeepot. But the pot was empty, and the counters were all clean. It didn't look like anyone was using the room.

I dropped into one of the chairs, shoved off my sandal straps, and let my shoes fall to the floor. I curled my achy feet under my legs and buried my face in my hands. Why couldn't life be more like the movies? In the movies, I'd have started my solo and a whole orchestra would miraculously have joined in. Tears would have flooded Hallady's eyes with the beauty of my playing. "I must have you in my band!" he would have cried.

A sharp click burst my movie-dream bubble. I looked up as the door handle turned. I grabbed my sandals and tried to stuff my feet back in. *Great. Busted.*

Only, it wasn't a hotel person who walked in.

It was Michael Malone.

Surprise flashed on his face when he saw me. He did a quick scan of the room. "You hiding out?"

"No." I let my shoes drop again. "I just wanted a little privacy. So . . . ," I added pointedly.

He ignored the hint and walked in, closing the door behind him.

"What are you doing?" I asked.

He headed for the fridge. "Is it locked?"

"I don't know." I twisted in my chair.

He tugged the door open—"Empty"—then circled back and dropped into the chair across from me.

"Don't you have somewhere else to be?"

"Not really."

"So why don't you find Lori?"

"She's auditioning soon." He stuck his feet on the table—there was a price tag on the bottom of his right shoe. He'd yanked his dress shirt out of his pants, and it hung down in a million wrinkles. A yellow-striped tie hung loose around his neck. He looked as relaxed and confident as he had that first day at the car wash. I'd hated him on principle that day. Now I just hated him.

"So how did your audition go?" he asked.

"Fine," I snapped. "How did yours go?"

Michael's audition had been scheduled for fifteen minutes after mine. He must have just finished.

"Great," he said. "No big deal."

"No big deal?" I repeated. *Could you stab a hole in someone's heart with a pair of two-inch heels?* "Then why don't you find Brandon and brag to him?"

"It's more fun to brag to you." He grinned, but I recognized a forced smile when I saw one. He scanned the room again, even though there was nothing to look at but framed pictures of blue and green squares.

And suddenly I knew. I just knew. "You bombed it," I said.

"I did not!" His eyes shot back to mine, but only for a second.

I sat forward. "Yeah, you did."

"You're the one who bombed it," he returned. "Why else are you hiding out?"

"I'm not hiding out."

"Then how did you do?"

I crossed my arms over my chest. "If you really want to know, I played well."

"*Well?*" he repeated, raising his eyebrows.

"Very well. Extremely well. In fact," I said, "Dr. Hallady smiled when I finished."

Michael grunted. "Now I know you're lying. That guy couldn't smile if you grabbed both sides of his mouth and stretched."

Startled, I met his eyes. And I realized that Hallady freaked him out, too. I looked away. I didn't want to be on the same wavelength as Michael Malone. "Whatever," I muttered.

"Maybe it just looked like a smile," Michael said, "because he was farting under the table." Then he launched his chair into a spin.

I straightened my dress over my knees and fought the urge to laugh. I wasn't a big fan of fart jokes, but Hallady tooting like a baby . . . yeah, that warmed my heart.

When Michael stopped spinning, I was smiling. And so was he. The smirk had disappeared, and it felt like a different guy sitting there. The Michael I'd gotten a peek at in the practice room. The one with friendly eyes, an easy smile, and a tiny face-scrunch line between his eyebrows. It was much harder to hate this version.

He stuck his feet back up on the table. "So does Hallady always look like that?"

"Pretty much."

"Was he wearing lipstick?"

"I don't think so," I said. "It's just because his skin is so white."

"White? I think the dude might glow in the dark."

"Lori thinks he's cool."

"In a freaky, creeper way," he said. "He stared the whole time I played. Like Dr. Freak-enstein."

"More like Count Freakula."

Our eyes met and I knew he understood. Maybe in a way no one else could have. "Did he ask you to repeat your name after you finished?" I asked.

"Yeah, what's up with that?"

"I don't know. He has our names on his clipboard."

"Did he write a lot while you played?"

I thought a minute. "I don't think so. Why? Did he write a lot for you?"

Michael's eyes dipped, and he shrugged.

A thought zinged from my tingling toes all the way to the ends of my curly hair. Michael was just as worried as I was. Worried because of *me*. Because he thought I was *good*. Why else would he want me to mess up? I don't know why I hadn't thought of that before, but I thought about it now.

And I liked how it felt.

Which one of us had done better? Which one of us would be on the list tomorrow? Which one wouldn't? The questions were like a lit match burning a hole inside me.

The fridge hummed a little, and the air conditioner kicked on with a whir. I strained to hear any outside noise, but there was nothing. Still, I knew that every fifteen minutes someone else headed into room 105 for their turn. Lori might be playing right now. I'd always been outside her room, waiting.

I picked at the edge of my thumbnail. "So will you tell me the truth about something?"

"What?"

"Was it really your idea to have me mess up? Or was it hers?"

He ran his fingers through his smoothly brushed hair, letting it fall into messy waves. "It was mine."

I glared at him in disgust. "You're a jerk, you know that?" But I couldn't work up any real anger. I was too relieved it wasn't Lori—I hadn't been completely sure. "I'm surprised you didn't just get her to dump my duet for yours."

"I tried," he said.

I gasped. "Seriously?"

"Yeah," he admitted. "You gotta do what you gotta do. It's a competition, right?"

"That doesn't make it okay."

"She didn't have to ask you. And you didn't have to say yes."

I leaned forward, curling my toes into the scratchy carpet. "It's still a crappy thing to do. And if you're as good as you say, you wouldn't have had to."

"I didn't have to. It was insurance."

"Liar." I eye-rolled him a heavy dose of disbelief. "You're as worried as I am. Admit it."

He shrugged.

"I don't get why. You played in a youth symphony. What's the big deal about middle school district band?"

His jaw tensed, but I couldn't read his eyes—they were focused on a patch of carpet. "The youth symphony was directed by my dad's friend. I got in without an audition."

"But . . ." I sat there a second with my mouth hanging open. "I was so freaked about that when you moved here, you have no idea." I blinked. "Wait a minute. Is your dad really a musician in New York?"

"Yeah." He looked up. "That part's all true. Too true," he added under his breath. "Music is all he cares about."

"Are you really going to go to New York to live with him?"

"I don't know. Maybe."

Or maybe not. That part Michael didn't say, but I could hear it in the silence that followed. If there was a plan, it was Michael's plan.

What would I do for a chance to be with my dad? I wondered. "Well, congrats. I bought the whole confident act," I said.

"My dad taught me that." He crossed one foot over his knee. "He says you fake confidence long enough and before you know it, it's not fake."

"And that works?"

He noticed the price tag on his shoe and picked at it with his fingers. "It works better on other people than it works on yourself." He peeled up half of the gummy tag. "Other people don't know you're faking—they see confidence and believe it. But you always know it's a show."

"It didn't seem like a show—you had me convinced."

"Hopefully, I convinced Count Freakula, too."

"Hopefully, you didn't."

He glanced up, but a smile twitched at the corners of his mouth. "Guess we'll find out tomorrow."

I smiled back. "Yep." Mr. Wayne had decided not to post results until the morning so everyone could enjoy the night. "Now we can all be too nervous to sleep."

"Except Hallady," Michael muttered.

"He'll be relaxing in his coffin."

Michael laughed. He flicked the tag off his fingers and onto the carpet. "So why'd you really decide to do a solo?"

I thought a minute. "I can't rely on Lori forever. If I want to keep playing, I'm going to have to do a solo sometime. And I want to keep playing."

We were both quiet then, and I felt relaxed for the first time in weeks. I wondered if I would like Michael now that we weren't enemies.

"So how did you do?" he asked suddenly. "Really?"

I hugged my middle and let out a sigh, thinking back. In the first horrible minute, I'd squeaked trying to shift to the upper octave. I'd winced. Even worse, Hallady had winced. But I hadn't freaked out. When I squeaked in the closet, I just started over. So that's what I did. I didn't ask for permission, or even look at him. I took a breath, and the second time through, I nailed it.

"I wasn't perfect," I told Michael. "But I was the best I could be." The words hung in the air a second, and I breathed them back in. Kind of amazing, really. I'd done a solo, and I hadn't exploded. Maybe I wasn't going to win any awards, but music had filled that room, and it had all been *me*.

"So how did *you* do. Really?" I asked.

His eyes flickered with uncertainty. "I played it solid. It's just . . . hard to know."

A low buzzing filled the room, and I looked around. Was it the air conditioner again? Then Michael dug in his back pocket, and I realized it was his cell vibrating.

He looked at the screen. "It's Lor. She finished. Went well." He typed something.

"She always kills at auditions," I said.

His phone beeped again, and he stood up. "I got to go. Oh—and she says she has the jeans she borrowed."

"Okay."

"Room 307," he added.

I nodded, even though I already knew. I still had the key card in my purse.

"You coming to the party later—room 382?"

"I don't know," I said. "Maybe."

He pulled open the door and stood there for a long second. "Good luck," he finally said.

I smiled. "Yeah. You, too."

♪ 28 ♫

I knocked on the door of room 307. No answer. I pressed my ear to the wall, and when I didn't hear anything, I slid the key card into the slot, pushed down the metal handle, and slowly walked inside.

"Lori?" I called out. "You here?" I smelled the jasmine body lotion she loved and saw her open suitcase, but no Lori. My jeans were there on the far bed—tucked under a pair of black sweats.

I stepped over pink flip-flops and a pair of inside-out shorts, then grabbed my jeans and took a quick look around. This was where I was supposed to be. My suitcase would have been next to Lori's, and our stuff would have been mixed together by now. In the bathroom, our makeup would have been spread out on the counter—my sweet-pea lotion next to her jasmine. I stopped as I faced myself in the mirror over the dresser. Lori and I would have stood here tonight getting ready.

How many times had we done that before? My mind crowded with memories. The year we both dressed up as black cats for Halloween and painted whiskers on each other's cheeks. The last day of fifth grade when we'd gotten our ears pierced and then stared at our reflections for nearly an hour wondering if we looked older. There were a million other times that weren't anything special—just us fixing our hair together or counting freckles or swapping lip-gloss colors.

My eyes filled, and my face wavered and blurred in the mirror. I used to blur my vision on purpose with Lori. I'd cross my eyes so that the edges of us over-lapped in the mirror and we looked like one person. Only now it was just me.

The lock clicked, and I hurriedly blinked my eyes as Lori pushed open the door.

"He-hey," I stammered, embarrassment rushing through me as her eyes widened and she froze in the entry.

"I got a key when I checked in—they just gave it to me. And I knocked, but you weren't here." I held up the jeans. "I came in to get these."

"It's okay," she said. "I'm glad you did." She walked over and set her flute case on the bed, pulling out the clip holding her bangs back. She'd twisted the rest of her hair into a bun like she always did. And I'd been with her a month ago when she'd bought the black dress. How did things change so much so fast? I squeezed the jeans to my chest, wishing I could stop thinking about everything from before.

"How did your audition go?" I asked.

She sighed and nodded. "Good. Great, even. How was yours?"

"Great. Really . . . great." Then I smiled to hide the fact that I didn't know what else to say. *How can I be with Lori and not know what to say?*

She ran her tongue over her lips, and I could tell she felt weird, too.

"Well, I should go," I said, moving toward the door.

"Tay."

Her voice stopped me, and when I looked over, her eyes were shiny.

"I'm glad you did great. Really, I am. I hope you make it."

"Thanks," I said, my voice suddenly thick. I could tell she meant it. But I thought she'd probably said the same thing to Michael and meant it then, too.

"And thanks for letting me wear your jeans."

"I said you could keep them—you really do look good in them." I paused. "I always thought you looked good—whatever size jeans you wore."

"Thanks." She swallowed. "I just didn't feel right keeping them. Not after . . . well, you know."

I hugged the jeans. "Yeah." I shrugged. "I'm sorry, Lori. I wish things had been different."

"I'm sorry, too," she said. "I never meant for any of this to happen. I thought we'd be best friends forever."

"I know," I said. "In some weird way, it's like you're still my best friend even if we're not friends anymore."

It didn't make sense—I knew that. But it was completely true. I couldn't erase our whole history after one weekend. It was like Andrew had said about Dad. I hated that shiny house of his and everything it meant, but it was still Dad.

I'd have to tell Aaron—if we ever spoke again—that I'd figured out something that doesn't change no matter what. The past. Nothing could mess up the way things had been—not even the way things had turned out now.

Lori wrapped her arms around her middle. "I'm sorry I got so mad."

"I'm sorry I couldn't do what you wanted."

"I should never have asked."

"No," I agreed, "you shouldn't have."

She paused a second. "Can we just forget that I ever did? Can we erase it, call a do-over, and go back to how things were?"

And that, I suddenly realized, was the downside of the past being unchangeable. You could never erase what had happened—not completely. No matter how much I wanted to. "I think things are going to be different no matter what we do."

"Maybe," she said. "But *we* don't have to be different. We've been best friends for six years—we're Tay-Lo, right?"

For the first time, it hit me: for all these years, I'd depended on her, but she'd depended on me, too. Maybe she looked beautiful on the outside, but I knew her on the inside, and she didn't make friends easily—no easier than I did.

"This is stupid, isn't it?" she said suddenly. "The two of us fighting. Especially now—when we've been talking about this weekend forever." Her hands flew up. "That's it. You know what we're going to do? We'll go get your stuff, and then we're going to share the room like we planned."

"Lori—"

"Yes," she said, grabbing my wrist the way she always did. "You have to. That can be your bed," she said, pointing to the one next to the window.

I pulled free. "I'm not going to stay here tonight."

She blinked, surprised. "Why not?"

"Because we can't erase everything that happened."

She tossed her clothes off the bed and onto the floor. "There—it's all yours."

"Lori, no," I said. "Things have to be different."

She paused at my voice, which had jumped at least three decibel levels. "What things?"

"For one, you asked me to screw up my audition!"

"And I would never do that again," she said.

I rubbed a hand around my neck. "It's not just that."

"Then what?" She sat down, kicking off her shoes. "I'm listening."

I took a breath. *Okay. What?* I sat down on the opposite bed. "Well, for starters, you can't blow me off for your boyfriend. I mean," I added, "you can, but I'm going to be mad about it."

"I never said you couldn't get mad."

"But when I do, you act like you'll never talk to me again."

She looked down and gave the tiniest of shrugs. "Okay, so maybe I do that sometimes. But now that I know," she said, meeting my eyes, "I won't do it anymore. What else?"

"Band," I said.

"What about band?"

"I think I can be good."

"I never said you couldn't."

"But you act like it."

"Because you act like it," she shot back. "You're the one always saying you stink. Or that you shouldn't try for Wind Ensemble."

I opened my mouth to argue, but this time I had to look away. She was right. "Well, I'm not going to do that anymore. I'm going to keep playing—no matter what happens tomorrow morning."

"You should," she said. "Maybe you can join my summer ensemble group."

"I'm not sure—"

"Or we'll find a music camp." She gestured with a hand for me to keep going. "What else?"

I paused a second and then laughed. "Whatever I say, are you just going to agree?"

"No." She smiled. "See?"

I sighed. "I can't believe we're finally talking about all this."

"And I can't believe we're not *done* talking about it," Lori said. "Because you could have had your suitcase by now. We could be out of these stupid dresses and getting ready for a party." She got up and slid her feet into her flip-flops. "Come on. I'll go with you to get your stuff."

And it was so much like before, like it had always been, that I almost stood up and let her lead the way.

But I was done following.

"We're not going to get my stuff."

She turned back around with a frown. "You want to borrow something? I brought the purple shirt you like."

"No." I took a deep breath. "I'm not going to stay here tonight—I told you."

"But that was before we worked everything out."

"This is part of me working stuff out."

"Staying with Kerry and Misa?" She rolled her eyes. "That doesn't make any sense. Come on, Tay." She strode back and leaned down to grab my wrist.

Before she could, I tucked my hands under my arms, stiffening as her eyes narrowed in a frown.

"I don't get it—what's the problem?"

I sighed, not sure how to explain. But if I stayed, I'd

let her grab my wrist and not only that, but I'd *like* it—it was easy just to go along and trust Lori to know where we were headed. And I'd lie in bed and measure my breath to hers, and I'd stand next to her in front of the mirror and blur my vision until I'd blurred the edges of myself. I'd fall back into Tay-Lo and the perfectness of having a best friend. It would be just like it always was—the way I always wanted it to be. Except somewhere in the past few weeks, something unexpected had changed.

Me.

I didn't want to be Tay with a hyphen—and least, not all the time. I wanted to have a best friend, but I wanted to be my own best friend, too. That meant I had to stand my ground.

Starting tonight.

"I'm going to go," I said. I grabbed the jeans and stood, but she held up her hand, stopping me.

"Seriously?"

"Seriously."

She twisted her fingers together, and there was a hesitant look in her eyes I hadn't seen before. "Okay. If that's what you want to do. But just because you're sleeping in a different room doesn't mean we can't hang out together, does it?"

Relief filled me, rising from my toes up my spine and to the tips of my ears. "I guess not," I said, half laughing. Warm gushiness filled me, and there was no way I was going to put that into words. So instead, I reached over, grabbed Lori's wrist, and pulled her into a hug.

When we broke apart a minute later, we both laughed.

"So we're okay?" she said. "Just like before?"

Not just like before. I wasn't going to forget what happened. But I still nodded.

Because I was pretty sure that we were going to be okay.

"Come on, we have to go!"

Our truce had lasted all of three hours. Enough time for us to change out of our dresses, eat a bag of rice cakes, and watch part of a *Buffy* marathon. Now Lori stood over me, hands on her hips, giving me the evil eye.

"I'm not going to that party," I said.

"You're the one who wanted to go in the first place," she reminded me.

"That was before."

"Is it because Brandon is rooming with Michael?"

"It has nothing to do with Michael."

Her eyes widened suddenly. "Aaron."

Just his name made my stomach churn like Dad's new mixer. I rolled off the bed and onto my feet. "I'm leaving," I said. "I'll see ya later." I sidestepped left, toward the door.

She sidestepped right, blocking my way. "Come clean," she demanded. "What's the deal?"

"I thought you weren't going to be so bossy."

"I'm not being bossy. I'm being a concerned and interested friend." She flashed me a "so there" smile.

"Fine," I said. "I'm not going because Aaron will be there. With Steph," I added pointedly.

"So?"

"So I don't want to watch her giggle and flip her hair every five minutes."

I stepped to my right just as Lori stepped to her left. A best friend who could read your mind had a definite downside.

"Because you still like him?" she asked.

"As a friend. Strictly Level One."

"Yeah, right," she said, while her eyes beamed "liar." "If you just like him as a friend, then why not come to the party?"

"Because we had a fight, and I feel stupid about it. Now, would you let me get by?"

"No," she said, brushing off that idea with a wave of her hand. "Say you're sorry, and tell him you still like him. He still likes you."

I sank back down on the bed. "He does not. He won't even talk to me."

She sat across from me. "That's proof he *does* like you."

"It is not."

"I've had a boyfriend for three weeks," she said. "I'm practically an expert on these things."

I smiled. "I wish it were that easy."

"Why can't it be? If you can do a solo for Hallady, you can talk to Aaron."

I flopped flat on my back. "It's different."

"So you're wimping out?"

"I'm not wimping out." I shot up to my elbows. Then I paused. *Was I?*

I couldn't just walk up to Aaron and tell him I was sorry. Except, that uh, yeah, I could. "Can't" is what we tell ourselves when something is hard. My mom's words repeated in my head just as clear and annoying as if she were there in person.

"This is impossible," I fumed. "He's hanging out with Steph now. They're playing Sudoku together."

"But you're the one he likes."

"You don't know that."

"There's one way to be sure," she said. "Come to the party and talk to Aaron."

"And risk public humiliation and shame?"

Lori grinned. "Exactly."

I sighed. "Life was much easier when I was a wimp."

♪ 29 ♫

From the sound of things, the party was in full swing when Lori and I got there. A muted hum of voices and music filled the hallway. We paused outside the door to take a breath and do a last-minute beauty check.

In the end, Lori had worn the purple shirt, and I'd borrowed a lacy maroon cami. My hair was still in a bun, but Lori had pulled curly pieces loose around my ears and neck. I looked very cool in a messy-diva kind of way.

Michael and Brandon's room was exactly like ours, only the carpet had blue swirls and ours had green. They'd plugged an iPod into a speaker and hip-hop music thrummed around all the voices. There must have been thirty kids. Lori and I both hovered near the door, trying to take it all in. José and some of the other percussion guys were sitting on one bed with a big bowl of Cheetos. On the other bed, Tanner, Frank, and Brandon were laughing about something. One of the dressers had been shoved out of the way, and a group of kids sat on the carpet.

My heart paused in midbeat. Aaron sat in the circle with his back to me.

"Hey, you made it."

I turned to see Michael walk up and slide an arm over Lori's shoulder. She blushed and smiled, her eyes flickering to mine for just a second. It was easier to feel happy for Lori now that I could actually see what she'd gained—without worrying so much about what I had to lose.

"What's everyone doing over there?" I asked, gesturing to where Aaron sat.

"Seven in Heaven," Michael replied.

Even as he said the words, the closet door opened and Kevin and Jamie came out, blinking and grinning. From the bright red splotches on Jamie's cheeks and the stupid grin on Kevin's face, I'd say the two of them had done more than talk during their seven minutes. You didn't have to kiss in the closet, but that was the idea. Hardly anyone stayed in the whole seven minutes, but everyone came out looking embarrassed. Melanie and Jenny were arguing over who got to spin next.

Lori nudged my shoulder. "You gonna go over?"

I shook my head, my heart in my shoes. Steph sat

next to Aaron, so close they looked together. As in *together.* "I'm going to head to Angie's room."

As if she'd heard me, Steph looked up and flipped her straight brown hair over one shoulder. Then she flashed me a victory smile.

"Did you see that?" Lori asked.

"As if I care," I muttered. But I did.

"My turn to spin," Steph said loudly.

What? A shot of anger curled my fingers into fists. So she could take Aaron into the closet? *Over my dead body.*

"Huh?" Michael asked.

Oops—had I said that out loud? My face flushed, but my fists stayed clenched. "He hasn't even broken up with me. Not to my face," I said. "How can he go into the closet with another girl when we're not officially done?"

Fired up, I strode to the circle. Melanie was fighting with Steph over who got to spin. I squatted down next to Jenny and tapped her shoulder. "Scoot over."

She grinned and made room. I sat down but stayed on my knees.

"I go next," Melanie said.

"I called it first," Steph countered.

While both of them were locked on each other, I leaned forward and grabbed the bottle. They sputtered in surprise.

"Tay—wait your turn," Melanie said.

"I've got the bottle, so I guess that makes it my turn."

Steph lunged forward to steal it, but Jenny blocked her arm. "Go for it, Tay."

I smiled at Jenny. *Thanks!*

Before anyone else could stop me, I spun the bottle. Truthfully, it was more of a point than a spin so that when it stopped, the neck faced Aaron.

His hair gleamed with shades of red and brown as he pushed it off his forehead. He stared at the bottle like he couldn't figure out what it was doing pointing at him.

Steph knew. Her eyes flared at me.

"Go, Aaron," Michael said. He and Lori had come to watch.

I stood, stumbling over my feet. I ignored the questioning look Aaron shot me. Instead, I stepped into the closet, backed up to the far corner, and waited. A second later, he followed me in. Then someone slid the door shut behind us.

There was no going back now.

♪ 30 ♫

I didn't expect it to be so dark. Or so quiet. Or so smelly.

I sank to my butt and wedged myself in the corner. A strip of light leaked in through the bottom of the door, but it was no wider than a piece of dental floss. There was nothing but carpet under my fingers, and the hangers were empty above me. I knew because I'd bumped them with my head. I just didn't know what the smell was from. Hopefully, past loads of dirty laundry and sweaty shoes. And not, say, a dead mouse.

I tried to slow my breath. Inside the closet, it sounded like I'd just run a mile. I couldn't see Aaron; my eyes were still adjusting. But I could tell he'd sat in the opposite corner.

If only I could tell what he was thinking.

Had Tanner started the timer? I rubbed sweaty palms over my jeans. I'd felt pretty brilliant a minute ago—I'd gotten Aaron in a quiet place and we were alone (except for the potentially dead mouse) and I could say what I wanted to. Only how could I say anything with a clock ticking, a group of kids catcalling, and the vision of hair-flipping Steph outside waiting to shove a knife in my back?

"So what's going on?" Aaron asked. His voice made me jump. My elbow banged the wall.

"Did you forget I was here?" he asked, his voice dry.

Can he see me or just hear me? I licked my lips. "I wanted to talk to you."

"And what? You lost my number?"

"No, I didn't lose your number." I felt a spark of anger, which was good. I wasn't coordinated enough to worry and be angry at the same time. "I have two things to say, and then you can go back to the party."

"Fine. Then say them."

"Fine," I snapped in return. "One, I'm sorry. And two, I think it's lame for you to date someone new when you never officially broke up with me."

There was a long moment of nothingness. Then he said, "Sorry for what?"

So much for a denial that he wasn't dating Steph. I took a careful breath. "Sorry for everything, I guess."

"Could you be more specific?"

I controlled the urge to kick him in the leg. "I'm sorry for asking you out on a fake date. I'm sorry for getting mad at the bookstore. I'm sorry for being so stupid about Lori when you were right the whole time. Is that sorry enough?"

"That probably covers it."

I strained at the darkness. "You know, you could say you're sorry, too."

"For what?"

"For walking out of the bookstore. For ignoring me in science. For moving up in band and not even telling me." I curved my arms around my knees. "For someone who supposedly liked me, you sure got over it fast."

"Who says I got over it?"

Goose bumps sprung up on my arms. Suddenly, I was glad it was so dark. "You're acting like it with Steph."

"Did I say we're going out?"

"You didn't deny it just now."

I heard him shifting on the carpet. "So is that why you grabbed the bottle? So I could break up with you to your face?"

I swallowed. "Why? Do you want to?"

"Do you want me to?"

I rolled my eyes in frustration. "No. I don't," I said honestly. "But I would like to know why you won't even talk to me."

"Maybe I didn't feel like competing with Lori."

"I'm sorry about that, too," I said. "I didn't mean for it to be like that." I swallowed again, wishing my throat didn't feel like sandpaper. "And it won't be. Again. I mean, if there ever is another again." My face burned with embarrassment. I covered my cheeks with my hands, worried that I might start glowing. "I mean, unless you and Steph . . . You know . . ." My words trailed off.

"You mean do I like her?"

"Well, it's obvious she likes you," I said. "She flips her hair every time you get within two feet."

My eyes had finally adjusted enough that I could make out the shadow of his smile. "So is that the sign?" he asked. "I know a girl likes me if she flips her hair?"

"Except for me. If I tried to flip my hair, I could maim someone."

His smile widened. "So how do I know if *you* like me?"

"Jeez, Aaron." My heart seized up. "When a girl asks a guy to a closet, it's because she likes him."

His head dipped, and I could see him yanking at a thread of carpet. "Are you just saying all this because you and Lori aren't friends anymore?"

"No," I said. "We are friends again. But it's different now." I leaned my head against the wall. "I depended on Lori too much—you were right about that. Then she started changing, and I got worried that she didn't need me for a friend like she used to . . . which made me feel like I needed her even more." I drew in a breath. "So I said yes to Lori and no to you, and I forgot how to listen to myself. But I won't do that again. In fact," I said, "I'm going to speak up for what I want, even if it means dragging someone into a closet to do it. So," I added, my heart racing, "I like you, Aaron. I'd like to hang out with you. And if you still want to go out, great, but if not—"

"I never stopped."

He said it so fast, I wasn't ready. "Oh," I said weakly. "Well." My cheeks registered a thousand degrees again. "Good."

I heard him shift before I saw him, but then he slid forward. I could see the slant of his jaw, the glow of his eyes. He wasn't smiling now.

"So if I tried to kiss you, would you freak out again?"

"I didn't freak out."

"Tay," he said softly.

And I stopped arguing and closed my eyes.

It was like before, only not so fast. His lips were soft on mine and so warm I felt it like a flush on my skin. His hands slid over my shoulders and—

The door flew open with a bang. I jerked back, the light stinging my eyes.

Tanner gaped at us. "I thought you guys were just friends?"

I scrambled up and pushed past him, Aaron right behind me.

"You thought wrong," Aaron said. And he grabbed my hand.

♪ 31 ♫

By the time Mr. Wayne walked into the ballroom at 8:00 a.m., a crowd had gathered, most of us with red eyes and pillow hair. I stood in a quiet circle with Kerry, Misa, and Lori. We'd pulled on crumpled T-shirts, sweat-pants, and flip-flops. Aaron had joined up with Michael, Tanner, Brandon, and José. Tanner had a stack of three doughnuts in one hand while he stuffed a fourth into his mouth. There was a continental breakfast set up in the lobby, but I hadn't wanted to eat.

Mr. Wayne smiled as he walked past. "I hope you all had a wonderful evening."

I snuck a look at Aaron and caught him smiling at me. A tingle worked its way down to my bare toes. Aaron had been right about one other thing—there really was great star-watching out here.

I'd gotten back to the room before midnight curfew,

but just barely. Kerry and Misa were just getting in bed—Kerry had offered to share with me because Misa kicks like a dolphin when she sleeps—we call her Flipper. Lying in the dark, I'd told them the whole closet story, in detail, which was like watching a favorite movie for the second time—it's even better because you're not worrying about how things will turn out.

The Lori stuff was more complicated. I tried to explain why we'd made up but I was still in their room. At least I had auditions to distract them, and we ended up talking for a long time about how each of us had done.

Even though I should have been tired, I woke before the alarm went off and watched the clock tick through the minutes. Finally, we'd gotten up, and met Lori to come down to the ballroom.

"Remember, checkout is at ten," Mr. Wayne said. "You need to make sure I mark you off my sheet before you leave with a parent." He opened a folder in his hand and pulled out a single piece of paper—the list of who made it.

And who didn't.

I waited for a panic attack, but nothing. The new me was thinking positive.

Either that, or I was so tired my nerves were numb.

Mr. Wayne tacked the sheet to a display case and then fought his way out as everyone surged forward. I went left and hit a wall of tuba players. I tried shifting right, but the crowd was at least three people thick. No

way I could read the print from here. I'd gotten separated from my friends, and I still couldn't find a way in.
Then I felt a hand grab my elbow. I turned.

Michael gave me a half smile. "Come on. Might as
well see it together."

He shoved his way to the front, pulling me along
with him. I stepped on someone's foot and took an elbow
in my ribs. But then we were at the case and there it
was—the list of names typewritten on smooth white
paper. It was broken into sections. Flutes, Saxophones,
Trumpets—I lowered my eyes to the subheading: Clarinets. *There.*

Aaron Weiss. Angela Liu. Brooke Hart.

I blinked.

I read through the list again. I searched under French
horns and tubas and trombones. My name . . . where
was my name?

"Brooke freaking Hart?" Michael muttered.

I read the names for a third time, and finally it sank
in. My name wasn't there. Neither was Michael's.

"Everyone said she'd be out of town," he growled.

"She was," I said. "She is, I mean." I rubbed at my
face, a little dazed. "Something must have changed.
She never said."

I didn't make it.

Around us, more bodies pressed to get close. I
shoved people away, suddenly claustrophobic. I needed
to breathe. And maybe, to cry. I fought my way free

and stood there a second, frozen. From the corner of my eye, I saw Aaron looking for me. I didn't want to talk to him yet—I needed some time. I needed to breathe.

I couldn't *breathe.*

I rushed to the nearest door and shoved it open. Warm air hit me. The smell of flowers and grass. A flagstone walkway angled to the right of a fountain that gurgled and splashed drops of water on the path. My eyes had blurred with unshed tears, but I didn't need to see where I was going. I just needed to *go.*

I wiped at my eyes and let the path lead me away from the ballroom.

I didn't make it. After all of that, how could I have not made it?

If Lori had done the duet with me.

If Michael hadn't moved here.

If I'd started practicing my solo sooner.

If Hallady wasn't so scary, I wouldn't have been so nervous.

If. If. If.

The word swirled around my brain as tears trailed down my cheeks. What did any of it matter? I'd tried everything I could. I'd pictured Hallady in footie pajamas. I'd practiced so much I had a permanent callus on my thumb, and my bottom lip was now the biggest muscle in my body. I'd done everything Mr. Wayne had said, and even playing to my strengths, I just wasn't good enough.

Somehow, I'd forgotten that fact while I'd been so busy practicing and thinking positive and visualizing good things.

As if that actually works.

A crunch of gravel startled me. I looked up just as a man appeared from a bend in the path. I sucked in a breath. Hallady.

Dr. Freakula.

He walked with his hands clasped behind his back and his white pointy chin in the air. His black sneakers hit the flagstone in measured, rhythmic steps while his dark sunglasses reflected sunlight like two mirrors. Had he stayed the night? Or had he come back to watch the effects of his dirty work?

He likes to see kids cry. Hadn't someone said that about him? I stepped off the path and kept my head down so he could pass by. But as soon as his shoes came into view, he stopped.

I looked up. The mirrors focused on me.

"Miss Austin, is it?" he asked.

My heart slammed against my ribs. I nodded, my throat clogged with new tears.

"I assume from your expression that Mr. Wayne has posted the results for District Honor Band."

No duh.

"It's a shame that not everyone can make it," he said then, his voice so cold and snooty. "But hard work is the answer."

In the split second it took for his words to sink in, I lost it. Completely, totally, lost it. It was as if I'd been standing on a cliff and with one little finger, Hallady had just pushed me off the edge. Rage screamed through me. Maybe I hadn't been the best player. Maybe I wasn't a natural. But I'd worked my butt off, and I was too tired and upset to put up with a lecture from a pointy-faced vamp.

"You want to know something?" I bit out, my hands on my hips, my fingers balled into fists. "I *did* work hard. I put everything I had into this audition." I stuck out my right thumb. "Just look at that! I dare you to find a clarinetist in there with a bigger callus."

He slid the sunglasses off his face and blinked at my shaky thumb. "Impressive."

Is he making fun of me? Tears sprang to the corners of my eyes. I knew I was out of control, but I couldn't stop myself. "If all it took was hard work, then my name would be on that list."

"If you had let me finish, Miss Austin, I wasn't faulting your work ethic. In fact, I applaud it." He looked down at the thumb I still had shoved in his face. "And your callus," he added drily.

I stuck my hand behind my back.

"I spoke with Mr. Wayne about your situation. He explained your last-minute switch to a solo and your dedication to your instrument. I commend you. Performing a solo is an important step for every musician and especially important for those who wish to continue to play."

"But"—I swallowed and stared at the top button of his shirt; that was about the only part of him that wasn't scary looking—"I didn't make the band."

"No," he said. "Your performance had merit, but in the end you came up short."

And this was Dr. Hallady being *nice*?

"However," he added, "I was impressed with your musicality and expression. And you demonstrate a certain fearlessness that I respect."

Fearlessness? Me? I looked into his eyes. They were an ugly dark gray—but at least they weren't red or flaming.

"Not many would dare to confront me. I like confidence in my students."

I hoped he also liked slack-jawed idiots, because that's what I felt like. *Fearless* and *confident?*

"Your performance wasn't quite there this time. But you do get credit for effort, Miss Austin. It seems that you may have potential if you plan to continue."

"I do," I said breathlessly. "Plan to continue."

He slid his sunglasses back on. "If you work hard enough to double the size of that callus by August, you may call my office and arrange an audition before school begins. I will be making the final list for Wind Ensemble at that time."

I broke into a smile. "Thank you. I will."

"Now," he said, "if you'll kindly step out of the way."

And he proceeded on, his arms still behind his back, his shoes slapping the ground in precise steps.

I stared after him until he was gone. *Me, Wind Ensemble?* I couldn't wait to tell Aaron and Lori and Kerry and Misa and Mom and Dad and *everyone.* Hard work paid off. Just like I'd always known.

And, I thought with a grin, *it didn't hurt to be fearless.*

♪ 32 ♫

The Desert Rose Nursing Home had spared no expense for the production of *Harry and the Heiress.* The assembly room couches had been pushed back, making room for five rows of folding chairs and a space in front for wheelchairs. Someone had thrown a sheet over the vending machine, and the TV screen was covered with a sign that said QUIET! UNWRAP COUGH DROPS NOW BEFORE THE SHOW BEGINS. Gray shower curtains hung from rods, hiding the raised platform stage. A CD player balanced on the edge of a folding chair, and scratchy piano music filled the room.

In other words, it was majorly lame.

"Sorry," I said to Aaron as we stood at the doorway. "It's not exactly Broadway."

He slid his hand into mine, and I wrapped my fingers through his, loving the scratchy feel of his palm. It was

Friday night, less than a week since Band Night Out. Having a boyfriend still felt new and unreal sometimes.

He looked so good in black jeans and a white polo that I kept sneaking glances at him. I'd straightened my hair and worn a dress. Mom insisted Andrew and I look nice for the theater. Technically, this shouldn't count, since it was a dress rehearsal at a nursing home, but I didn't argue.

Andrew leaned in from just behind me and said, "We dressed up for *this*?"

"Quiet," Emily said. I heard Andrew grunt, which meant she'd just jabbed him with an elbow. Emily Moira, Andrew's girlfriend and lover of the smelly musk, had a way of keeping him in line.

Except when it came to the chin hair.

Adobe's baseball team was now seven for their last seven games. Playoffs started next week, and the Beard had become the team's good-luck charm. Andrew's chin hair had continued to grow with the disgusting addition of a kink near the bottom. As if the hair had reached a certain length and taken a sharp right turn.

"This is sweet," Emily said. "Look at how excited these people are."

"They're a hundred years old; they get excited about bowel movements," Andrew said.

I turned in time to catch her glare at him. "Do you want me to pull that hair? Because I can."

"It's not a hair," he said. "It's a full beard, and you're not coming near it."

"I wouldn't want to," she returned. Then she gave Aaron a measured look. "I hope you're not planning on growing one of those things."

"It's not the kind of thing you plan," he replied.

"Jealous," Andrew said, "you're all jealous." He ran his fingers beneath the so-called beard, as if you could fluff up one hair.

Emily rolled her beautiful brown eyes. "Don't you have a job to do?"

Andrew shifted the camera bag on his shoulder. "Guess I'd better set up. You wanna kiss my beard first?"

"Gross," she said, shoving his chest with one hand. "Go."

Andrew had just finished a multimedia class, which apparently qualified him to be the official videographer for the production. Yesterday, the playwright had dropped off an old-school camera and a tripod so Andrew could "practice." Of course, he'd never unzipped the case.

We followed him down the back row of chairs until he reached the middle aisle, where he took the end seat and set up the tripod. Emily sat next to him, then me, then Aaron. People turned in their chairs to look at us, smiling and nodding with watery blue eyes. Did everyone's eyes fade to blue when they got old?

I settled in, missing Dad only a little. Mostly, I missed the idea of him—and us—as a family. It made me sad to think that we would never be one again—at least not like before. But it was getting easier. And when Andrew went to spend the night this past Tuesday, I went with him.

I ran a hand over the gold charm bracelet around my wrist. Dad had flown to China two days ago, but he'd left the velvet jewelry box for me. When I opened it, I found the bracelet with the heart charm, but a new message had been engraved: FEARLESS. I hadn't taken it off since.

The music stopped, and there was a buzz in the room as everyone hurried to sit down. "This camera is ancient," Andrew muttered, holding it up to show Emily. "There's no display. I'm going to have to focus through the eye piece."

"You'll look like a movie director."

"Yeah?" Andrew thought for a second and then grinned. "Cool." He leaned in to attach the camera to the tripod, and I looked up front, wondering if Mom stood behind the shower curtain, waiting for her cue. This might not be Broadway, but she'd still been a nervous wreck all week. I'd come down for a snack yesterday and caught her pacing around the kitchen island murmuring, "Your love may never die, Harry, but you will. Back away and drop the cane."

It was her big line in the play when her true identity

was revealed. Yesterday, Andrew had startled her in the garage, and she'd spun around and yelled, "Drop the cane!"

Looking now at the old people—at least two of them were snoring—I didn't see what she had to worry about. They weren't exactly theater critics. But at the same time, I kind of understood. This audience was Mom's Dr. Hallady—only with hearing aids and gargling coughs.

I looked up as a short woman in a flowery dress and black loafers walked to the center of the room. "Welcome," she said. "Thank you so much for joining us for this sneak-peek performance of *Harry and the Heiress.* I'm Anita Weebans, the playwright, and I do hope you'll enjoy the show. And now, with no further ado."

She slid back the shower curtains, the metal rings clanging as she revealed the set. It wasn't much: one easy chair on the left, a patio chair on the right, and a folding screen set up between them to represent a wall between indoors and outdoors. A huge square had been cut out of the screen for a window.

A minute later, there was Mom in her getup as Nurse Welty. She tucked a shawl around the shoulders of a white-haired lady and helped her to the easy chair on the left. I recognized the old woman as Mom's friend Mrs. Lansing, who had been decked out in a white wig, pearl necklaces, and rings as shiny (and as big) as mirrors. Way better costume than a nurse.

"You have thirty minutes until lunch," Mom/Nurse

Welty said. I wondered if Andrew was catching Mom's foot on tape. When she got nervous, she tapped her foot. Right now, it was going so fast the hem of her nurse dress fluttered. "I'll leave you to enjoy the view."

Someone in the audience burped and someone else coughed. Andrew leaned forward, the camera pressed to his face, as an old guy playing Harry walked on, his cane hitting the floor with each heavy step. He lowered himself in the patio chair and sighed. "I'm Harry Adelman," he said. "Just moved in."

Margaret, the heiress, turned her head just enough so you knew she was ignoring him.

"Nice view," Harry said.

"It was," she said stiffly.

Then I got caught up as Harry charmed Margaret into talking and then flirting. The man playing Harry was good—funny. Before too long, he and Margaret were meeting at the window each day. The first act ended as Harry proposed marriage and Margaret accepted. Then Nurse Welty took center stage—she had the last line of the act, and my heart thumped a little as she held a flip phone with one hand.

"Don't worry," she promised, pretending to talk into the phone. "Your mother will never marry that man. I'll end the romance. Permanently, if I have to." Then, she held up a loaded syringe and pressed the plunger just enough to let out a spray of liquid. The audience gasped, then broke into applause.

It was kind of . . . well, it was good. *Mom* was good.

By the second act, her foot had stopped shaking completely, and her voice seemed stronger as she plotted Harry's demise while keeping her secret identity secret.

Andrew had his face glued to the camera as her big moment came.

"Your love may never die, Harry, but you will," she said. Then she bent over and yanked up her skirt.

What?

A leather holster strapped tightly to her thigh—a gun gleamed at the top. I groaned, but the sound was drowned out by gasps. Around me, the audience's attention was glued to the stage. To Nurse Welty, Secret Bodyguard. Mom's voice dripped venom. "Back away and drop the cane."

Goose bumps ran down my arms. More than a few people slapped hands to their mouths.

A funny feeling worked its way through me. I was . . . proud. *Of my mom.*

Of course, it turned out that Harry had been in special forces a century ago, and he unarmed Mom with a fancy twirl of his cane. The play ended as Harry leaned toward the window and Margaret leaned toward the window. I held my breath like everyone else, waiting for the kiss . . . waiting. . . .

A sudden scream of pain echoed through the room. I jerked, startled, then horrified. It wasn't a random scream—it was Andrew.

As if Mom had recognized his shriek, the curtains flew open and she ran out—right through the nearly kissing Harry and Margaret. "Andrew?" she called.

He jumped up while everyone turned to stare. His face had frozen in terror, his eyes locked on something in the palm of his hand.

"My beard," he cried. "The camera yanked out my beard!"

Mom stopped short, her chest heaving as she took a long breath.

And next to me, with a huge smile, Emily stood up and began applauding.

As if that were some kind of cue, everyone else joined in. Mom climbed back on stage as applause rocked the place. No one clapped louder than I did. I wasn't even sure what I was clapping for—Mom, Andrew . . . maybe just for life in general.

Finally, after a last bow, Mom raised her head and our eyes met. I flashed her a thumbs-up. She grinned, and even with purple makeup and smashed hair, I thought she looked beautiful.

Maybe this play stuff hadn't been so lame, after all.

But no way was she keeping that thigh holster.

♪ 33 ♫

Today, the cafeteria smelled like potatoes—a definite improvement over the usual aroma of mystery meat. I unwrapped my lunch bag while I half listened to Aaron and Brooke. They were arguing over who would win in a fight—a Ringwraith or a Death Eater. Aaron sat across from me, a fistful of cookies in one hand. Lori sat next to me, then Kerry, and then Misa. Across from them sat Michael, Brandon, and Tanner. Somehow, we'd taken over the whole table. A band table.

In the month since auditions, Lori and I had gone back to our usual routine. Kerry and Misa still called us Tay-Lo, we talked every day, and sent eye messages across the band room. She'd even slept over on Saturday night. Everything seemed the same, but it was different. I couldn't explain it exactly, but where we'd always been shoulder to shoulder—no room between us—there was just a little space now.

Maybe because I'd stopped leaning on her so much.

Mom's play had gone over so well, the cast had started touring retirement villages on the weekends. Half the time I came home to find Mrs. Lansing and the other cast members sipping coffee in the kitchen and reliving the latest performance. I still wished it were Dad sitting there, with his coffee mug and the place mat in his old spot at the table. But the house was always noisy and someone was laughing. Usually Mom.

My family of stars had shifted around some—but the Austin family constellation hadn't exploded. Maybe Dad's star had drifted farther out, but I knew he was still there. And now there were new stars—Emily, who had sewn Andrew's chin hair into the brim of his baseball hat and saved the entire season (according to Andrew), because without that hair he'd never have pitched so well in the playoffs. And Aaron, whose star had been there all along, if only I'd focused a little better.

Other things had changed in the last couple of weeks, too. For one thing, Michael had turned out to be okay. I'd told him about my talk with Dr. Hallady, and he was all fired up about auditioning, too. Since neither of us had made District Honor Band, he wanted to get together the weekend of the concert and have our own mini—practice camp. I thought maybe I'd say yes. Brooke felt bad about how things had turned out, but it wasn't her fault. Just bad luck. Her grandma had broken a hip, so her family had to cancel their trip back

East, which meant Brooke could participate, after all. And she'd made it, fair and square. But one day I was going to challenge her—and win.

I was still bummed about District Honor Band, but Wind Ensemble was my new goal. And I had more confidence now. I might still squeak with nerves, but I'd finally figured out that everyone worried as much as I did. Some kids just hid it better.

"I think a Death Eater would win," Brooke was saying. "I'm going to use that for my language-arts essay."

"You're wrong, but it'll make a good topic," Aaron said.

Brooke sighed. "Except I'm supposed to support my position. With facts."

"You could add up the number of fights they had in the movies," I offered. "Figure out the number of people each of them killed and who has the highest percentage."

Brooke's eyes widened. "Cool, but way over my math IQ."

I smiled. "I'll help. I'm good at that stuff."

Aaron grinned and bit into an Oreo.

"So we'll have to start thinking about Grad dance," Misa said, looking down the table to include everyone.

"We should go as a group," Kerry said.

"Or do you guys want to go as couples?" Misa asked, her gaze lasering in on Lori and then me.

"I don't need to go as a couple," I said.

"What?" Aaron kicked me under the table. "You're coming with me."

"Maybe."

"Maybe?"

I laughed at the look on his face. "Yeah," I said. "I am."

I wasn't afraid of going solo anymore. But sometimes it was still nice to be part of a duet.

♪ Acknowledgments ♫

With thanks to the many people who helped me bring this story to life.

To Caryn Wiseman, my wonderful agent, who saw an early draft and said, "I think you've got something good here . . ." To my insightful editor, Stacy Cantor Abrams, who always asked just the right questions—this would not be the story it is without you. To Mary Kate Castellani, for taking over with very capable hands, and to Katy Hershberger and the rest of the incredible team at Walker & Company.

To Kimberly Fellner, my talented niece, for reminding me of all the things I'd forgotten about middle school band. I did my best to stay true to the band experience, but for the sake of the story, I took liberties with the rules of District Honor Band. I hope band members will forgive me.

To the teens who read early versions and provided feedback: Kassidy McDonald and Alison Ochs. To Rachel, who read for me even though there were no vampires or demons, and to Kyle, who inspired the character of Andrew right down to the chin hair. (Some stuff you just can't make up.) To critique partners Marty Murphy and Anita Weiss, and the all-knowing Daphne Atkeson, who reads everything first and never leads me astray. To Gene Lauritano, who offered to read my first manuscript and turned out to be such a great editor, he's stuck with the job forever.

Hugs to the Class of 2k11—what would I have done without your support and wisdom? And, most especially, authors Kiki Hamilton and Gae Polisner, who also read parts of this book for me.

To Susan Fellner Schanerman, for all those Tuesdays at the bookstore, and to my extended family for cheering me on.

To everyone who read *OyMG* and asked for the next book—thank you!

Finally, to Jake, who never played an instrument, can't sing on key or find a beat, but who is always in-tune with me. I love you.